STORIES FROM THE STRANGE SIDE

JOSEPHINE MCCARTHY

PREVIOUSLY KNOWN AS
JOSEPHINE DUNNE

APOCRYPHILE
PRESS

Apocryphile Press
PO Box 255
Hannacroix, NY 12087
www.apocryphilepress.com

Copyright © Josephine Dunne, 1999; Margie McArthur, 2005.
Publication History: Samas Publishing, 2001; Black Bee/Sun Chalice Books,
2005; Margie McArthur/Faeriewood-by-the-Sea, 2005.
Printed in the United States of America
ISBN 978-1-965646-19-9 | paper
ISBN 978-1-965646-20-5 | ePub

Cover art by Ideogram AI.

Please join our mailing list at www.apocryphilepress.com/free. We'll keep you
up-to- date on all our new releases, and we'll also send you a FREE BOOK.
Visit us today!

Dedicated to Forrest

CONTENTS

ACKNOWLEDGMENTS

Thanks to Leander for her comments and reflections,
and to the strange man in Jerusalem.

CHAPTER I

FAERIES IN UNION SQUARE

MANHATTAN

West 19th Street shivered in a frosty blast of cold air that sneaked through people's jackets and nipped their ears. Peter hurried down the street and stood on the corner of 7th Ave, waiting for the traffic signal. His feet kicked against each other in an effort to try and encourage his circulation not to come to a total stop.

He looked in astonishment as people queued to get into the dance theater on the street corner. Everyone was huddled together as close as manners would permit in an attempt to escape the vicious cold wind.

The light finally changed to green and Peter shuffled across 7th Ave and down the last few feet to his home. His hand searched all the corners of his pockets even though he knew he had forgotten his key. Silent prayers bounced around Peter's head all the way to the front door in futile hope that Chris had not popped out for a minute, as was his habit.

He leaned his head against the door with his finger on the bell. No one came. He rested his head on the door not knowing what to do. "Maybe Chris has just gone out for a couple of minutes," thought Peter, "he often does that." He put down his briefcase and sat on it.

"I'll wait five minutes then go to the bar." The frost nipped his lips as he spoke out loud to the door.

Peter was very firm with himself. He sat looking up and down the street. It was empty. Only *he* was stupid enough to be out in this terrible weather. He put his nose into his gloved hands and breathed heavily in an attempt to warm his face up.

It was then that he saw something moving out of the corner of his eye—a strange silent shadow moving quickly past him. It was not small. Startled, he looked around quickly, but there was nothing there.

Almost immediately, the frost bit his nose. He had just buried his face back into his gloves when he heard someone call his name. He looked up, thankful and expecting to see Chris, but no one was there. His eyes scanned the street in both directions. Nothing.

He had just begun to worry that the cold was beginning to affect his mind when Chris strode around the corner waving to him. Peter stood up and looked at the tall man approaching him. He knew better than to tell Chris that he thought he was going nuts. Chris worried about everything.

Later that night, as Peter wrapped himself in the eiderdown, he thought he saw something move across the bedroom. A shadow flitted by and Peter sat up in bed, trying to see what was happening. The eiderdown moved with Peter as he sat up, creating a cold inrush that caught Chris and awoke him. Chris groaned against the cold.

"Sorry, I thought I saw something move, like a fast shadow." Peter lay back, looking at the ceiling. Maybe he was going nuts.

"This is Manhattan. It's full of fast shadows, now get to sleep before I put a pillow over your head."

Peter smiled into the darkness and turned over. Sleep pulled him quickly and before long he was snoring in chorus with Chris. He sank deeper and deeper into the blackness until someone whispered in his ear.

"Would you play for us Peter? Play, so that we may dance."

Peter dreamed he was playing his harp and that creatures were sneaking out of all the nooks and crannies of the city to come listen to his beautiful music. The dream became stronger and stronger as the faery beings danced around him while he played.

They were of so many different shapes and sizes. Some were dressed in eighteenth-century dress; some were clothed in bark and feathers. Others were part animal / part human looking.

One of the biggest, which looked like a large bear, came and sat beside Peter as he played. The faery being hummed along with the tune and began to cry. All the other faery beings stopped dancing and began to cry too. Soon, they were all weeping and Peter became very distressed.

"Why are you crying? What is wrong? Have I hurt you in some way?"

Peter was distraught with the thought that he may have done something to hurt these beautiful creatures. A faery woman, clothed in the dress of a settler and sporting bright red hair to her knees came and sat beside Peter and put her arms around him.

"No, Knight of the Music, you have but given us memories of a better time and place. See, watch, listen."

The woman placed her hands over Peter's eyes and she closed her own eyes. She started to tell him a story and Peter watched as he listened.

Peter began to see a scene unfold before him: Ocean mist

clung to his face as he looked out to sea. Trees bent in the sunshine and the sand moved, shifting beneath his feet as the tide clung to the shoreline. Tall ships dipped as the waves welcomed the strange visitors. Small white faces peered over the shipside while some waved banners and ribbons.

The land around Peter was forest. Deep, thick, sensuous forest that smelled of fresh earth and dew. Hiding in the forest were many faery beings clothed in twigs, bark and leaves. They looked at the ships with astonishment and wonder.

In among the people on the ship were faery beings darting from place to place, trying to see the approaching land. They were dressed as the humans were, but were shaped differently. Some were tall and thin; some were little and fat. Some glowed like the sun and some were chaotic like the wind. Others had the ocean in their eyes and some brayed like a donkey.

The faeries of the forest were excited. One by one they carefully crept forward out of the trees, once they were sure that the humans could not see them. They waved to the faeries on board the great ship, and the strange faeries waved back.

That evening, deep in the forest, the faeries held a gathering, making friends and exchanging gifts. They danced through the night and slept through the day, warmed by the sun and protected by the creatures of the forest.

The faeries of the forest were grateful to the humans for bringing these new friends, so they helped the humans learn about the seasons, the forest, the trees and the powers of the land. But the people were wicked and selfish. They stole more and more of the forest and did not heed the signs that nature sent as a warning of impending disaster.

They built and built until the forest was no more. The faeries were becoming homeless. They were forced to reside with the faeries of the Underworld who were good friends. But the Faeries of the forest missed the green and the dew.

Eventually the forest vanished under concrete, and the

underworld was damaged by poisons and by the strange powers that the humans used for energy. The faeries wandered the streets of the city, tending to any remaining trees and bits of grass that they could find. But the faeries were poor and in bad health.

The humans seemed to have put aside a little nature for the faeries, for in the city was a large park with water. But the humans had poisoned it by spraying things on the plants and adding death to the soil. The faeries could not bear to be there.

Peter thought his heart would break. He loved the city, but he had never realized before what a terrible price others had to pay for that. He wanted to do something, anything, no matter how small, to redress the balance.

He asked the woman if there was anything that he could do.

"Yes," she said and cupped her hands around his face. "Weep for us. Weep all you can and gather your tears in a chalice. Mix your tears with spring water and pour it into the cracks of the pavement. Water the land with your tears and you will give strength to the earth to fight back."

Peter began to weep. He wept as though his heart would break. Every pain he had ever suffered both physically and emotionally flowed through him as he wept. Something shook him. Something called his name.

Peter opened his eyes and realized he had been dreaming. Chris was shaking him and calling to him to wake up. Peter sat up in bed and looked around.

On his mantle shelf was a glass chalice that Chris had bought him when they first met. Peter sprang out of bed, still weeping, and grabbed the chalice. Chris sat up in bed in confusion asking him what on earth he was doing. Peter wiped the dust from the chalice and held it to his face. His tears dripped into the chalice and Peter wept.

Chris got out of bed and gently placed his hand on Peter's shoulder, looking at him in sorrow. Peter tried hard to catch each tear as it tumbled out of his eyes. He felt heartbroken, and could not stop crying. He tried to explain what was happening but it just sounded weirder and weirder, and after a while he grew silent. Chris padded out of the room and into the kitchen to put the kettle on. Tea always calmed Peter down.

A few moments later Peter came into the kitchen. He had stopped crying and was now hunting through all the cupboards while holding the chalice.

"Peter, what are you doing? It's three in the morning, and I'm freezing. What are you looking for?" Chris was hopping from foot to foot. The heating had failed again and his feet were like ice.

"I'm looking for spring water."

Peter did not look around at Chris as he spoke, his head buried in a cupboard.

"Dare I ask why you bounce out of bed, cry into a cup and then tear the place apart in the freezing cold at three in the morning looking for spring water? Or should I just go back to bed and pretend none of this happened? And by the way, there is a bottle of Evian on top of the fridge."

Chris stepped to one side as Peter dived for the water. He poured some into the chalice where he had wept and mixed the water with his tears.

He turned to look at Chris and smiled. "Just don't ask; really, you don't want to know."

Chris held his hands up in defeat and turned to go back to bed. Peter opened the coat cupboard and took out his boots and coat. He pulled a pair of jeans out of the dryer and struggled into them while trying to find a sweater.

"Peter, what, where are you going, what are you doing? Please, for God's sake!"

Chris was becoming alarmed. His partner was often strange: a visionary, a poet. But going out at three in the morning in this cold was just plain nuts. Peter put his arms on Chris's shoulders and looked straight into his eyes.

"There is something weird that I have to do. It's crazy, and I don't know why I'm doing it. But I am, so go to bed, and I will be back in a few minutes. Please, just let me do this, then I can get a good night's sleep."

Chris nodded and went back to bed. Peter, wrapped against the cold and holding on to the chalice, quietly crept out into the night and the cold. He walked down the street, looking at the pavement. He knew what he had to do. He poured his tears and the spring water into the cracks of the sidewalk up and down his street, a precious drop at a time. When the chalice was empty, he looked up and down the street before scurrying back to his warm bed.

He did not see Chris holding back the blind and watching him. He also did not see the bag lady hidden in the shadows as she smiled and nodded to him. She stood; her coat half open, oblivious to the cold as her eyes followed Peter's every move. She whispered something on the wind as he turned his back to her and climbed the steps to his apartment.

The following morning, the alarm shot though his head like a nagging mother, coaxing him out of his dreamless delicious sleep. When he had finally managed to get to sleep after his adventure, he had fallen down a hole of blackness that blocked out everything. Chris did not mention the night's madness and Peter decided it was best not to bring up the subject.

Peter was deep in thought as he stepped out onto the cold street that early spring morning, and had walked a few yards before his thoughts faded and his eyes focused on the sidewalk. Usually, it was covered with litter and feet, but no nature. This morning, little shoots of green poked out of the cracks in the concrete stretching towards the spring sun.

Peter looked around to see if anyone was watching. He

squatted on the sidewalk, looking at the green close up. There it was, jutting out of the concrete sidewalk, in the middle of Manhattan: a green army standing to attention in its infancy.

Nobody seemed to notice. Nobody pointed and looked at the little miracles being birthed in their midst. Everyone ignored them except Peter. He wanted to scream at people not to stand on them, not to destroy them. But he did not want to be hauled off for therapy, the ultimate torture, so he just stood and looked in astonishment.

The image stayed with him all through the working day and by that evening he knew what he wanted to do. He dashed home. Ignoring the fact that it was his turn to make dinner, he pulled out his harp and opened the window wide, letting the spring enter in all its cold glory. His fingers wove music that filtered out into the street below as he played to the green shoots that had dared to surface in the cold.

He wanted them to experience music before they died in the frost and songs surfaced in his thoughts as he played at random to the little miracles. He played and played until his fingers stiffened and his teeth began to chatter.

That night, as he drifted into sleep, he heard someone call his name. The voice was unearthly and he knew they had returned to him. As he fell deeper into sleep, the call became louder. He found himself on a grassy plain by a tall standing stone.

He sat down with his back to the stone and drank in the beauty of the landscape. The green grass lit the land rather than a sun or moon. Trees grew down from the sky, their branches lightly touching the grass below them and their roots dug into the dark sky above. Peter could hear people moving all around him, but he could not see them. He called out, but no one answered.

Something brushed against him and he spun around, but

saw nothing. The frustration built within him as he called and called for someone to appear.

"You have to find us by day, handsome bard, look for us by day..."

The words swirled around him as he stood up, leaning his forehead on the stone. "But how? But how?"

He shouted out across the empty landscape that he knew was full of faeries. Something tapped his shoulder and his eyes sprang open. Chris lay on his side with his head propped on his arm.

"You were shouting in your sleep. Are you feeling okay these days? Want to talk about it?"

Peter looked at Chris's concerned face for a moment and then shook his head. "No, it's okay. It's nothing, just the pasta."

Chris frowned. "What do you mean the pasta?" Then his face lightened into a smile. "Are you trying to tell me that my cooking is driving you nuts?"

He threw his pillow at Peter who dived under the eiderdown while trying not to laugh so loudly.

FOUR MONTHS LATER

Peter sat on the steps of his apartment looking at the weeds growing out of the cracks in the sidewalk. He was smiling widely as he held his newspaper. On the back page, in the local news, was a report about city cutbacks and the sidewalk clean up being cut back. It meant that no more chemicals would be sprayed across the sidewalk to kill the weeds.

An old woman shuffled down the street, pausing at every trashcan so that she could look through them for tidbits. Peter did not notice her until she was almost at his feet. He did not look up. The street people frightened him—not in a danger sense, but it was just something that he did not understand. He felt sorry for them but he was not sure how he should react to them.

She looked up at him and caught his eye. He was trapped. He smiled and looked away.

"You miss them, don't you?" she rasped. "Once they touch you, that is it. You can spend the rest of your life searching for them."

She shuffled on, not pausing for a response or a reaction. Peter thought for a moment and then realized that she was talking about the faeries. She must have been, what else would fit with such a comment?

He looked back down the street in the direction she had gone. He wanted to catch her and ask her how she knew and what did she mean. But the street was empty. There was nowhere else for her to go, and yet she was not there.

He ran to the end of the street and he breathed out in relief when he saw her waiting at the end of the next street, looking away from him. He ran towards her and she vanished around a second corner without looking back. He followed. She led him this way and that until he finally found himself in Union Square.

He stood on the corner and looked in all directions. He spotted her in the distance, standing outside a Buddhist restaurant. Once she saw him, she turned and vanished into the restaurant and Peter quickly followed. Now he was certain that she knew he was following her.

He got to the restaurant and climbed the stairs into the main part of the building. A quiet and peace descended upon him as he entered and he began to feel rather foolish. This was not the sort of place that a bag lady would enter; maybe he had been mistaken. He looked into every corner until it occurred to him that she might have sneaked into the rest rooms. A waiter stood and looked at Peter as he stared at the ladies' restroom.

"Would you like a table, sir?" The man asked politely.

Peter looked around him. There was a table that gave him a view of the bathrooms and the entrance. He went and sat at the table and the waiter gave him a menu. Peter did not know what to do. He felt embarrassed and realized he would have to order something. He asked for tea and a simple dish before settling with his eyes fixed on the restroom door. No one came in or out.

At first, he did not see the old man sitting at the next table. The man had long white hair and a thick beard that he constantly pulled. The man watched Peter with interest as Peter watched the door. Finally, the man came over to Peter's table and sat beside him.

"Young man, there is no one in there, I can vouch for that. I have been here for fifteen minutes and no woman has been in or out."

Peter looked at the man and realized he had made a fool of himself by staring at the restroom door.

"Are you sure? I mean, did you see an old lady, a street lady, go in there? A woman with a red scarf on her head and red gloves?"

The man pulled on his beard and smiled.

"Aha, that is why you will wait a long time. She will not come out of there because she is not in there. Funny how she led you here."

The man's voice was strange, with a foreign lilt to it.

Peter frowned. "How do you know? Do you know that woman? Who is she?" The man laughed and rubbed his hands together.

"I cannot tell you here. But I can tell you that you will want to hear what I have to say. Have you had strange dreams in the past few months? Hmm, thought so. Eat up, let me finish my soup and then you can come with me."

The old man returned to his seat, leaving Peter to stare at him in confusion. After they had both finished their meals, the old man stood up and put his coat on. Peter had been debating whether he should go with the old man or not. There were some strange people in the city and it would be just his luck to get picked up by a pervert or a maniac.

But there was something good about the old man's face, and he was very frail. Peter could snap him in two with his fingers if he wanted to. That finally clinched the decision for him. He was in no real danger.

Peter got up and left, walking as slowly as he could so as not to hurry the old man, who obviously found walking a problem. They moved at a snail's pace to a door around the corner. It did not look like a house or an apartment, but more like the service door of a shop or warehouse.

The old man fumbled with his keys and finally got the door open. Before them was a steep stairway which they climbed slowly, floor after floor, until Peter's legs grew tired. He marveled at the old man who slogged away without complaint, climbing up what must have felt like a mountain.

They emerged in a small apartment that looked as though it had been fashioned out of offices. It was full of books and clocks. Everywhere that Peter looked, there were books, dust and clocks. A loud noise came from the corner, which made Peter jump.

"Yes, yes, I'm back with your treats. Not so loud; you scare the natives."

The old man's voice seemed aimed at the noise, the source of which Peter was trying to see. In the corner, perched on a bookcase, was a large dark crow half hidden in the shadows.

"Peter, this is A.E. A.E., meet Peter."

The bird said hello and Peter nearly fell over in shock.

The old man laughed and the bird instantly imitated his laugh.

"I found him on the streets years ago, with wire around his leg and his wing half torn off. He has healed well, but he will never fly, so we two old farts live together. He loves his treats from the restaurant."

The old man unwrapped two steamed dumplings, which he put up on the bookcase. A.E. tucked into them with gusto, making lots of kissing and sucking noises as he lost himself in an orgy of Zen food.

Peter browsed the bookshelves, which were stuffed with every imaginable subject that would delight an inquiring mind. His fingers stopped at an old leather-bound volume on Faeries.

He opened the book and wandered through the text. The hairs on the back of his head pricked when he came to a passage marked "Faery Queen." He read the text under his breath as though his lips must echo the words that rolled around his brain.

"And though she be terrible, with her staring eyes and sharp teeth, and though she be fearful in her anger, the faery folk do delight when her heart is stolen. For then and only then dost she wear the clothing of a human form. But take heed, for when her love is a burning passion that draws man into the flame, then she does wear the look of an old and bended woman. And if the young man looks into her eyes and does recognize her, he shall fall with her to faeryland, never to be seen again. There he will reside in the land of richness and plenty."

Peter thought of the bag lady and then shook the silly thought out of his head. He put the book down and browsed some more. The old man watched him like a hawk, and A.E. watched him like a man.

"So, you be having some interest in the wee folk then young man?"

The old man's voice sang in the strange accent and A.E. mimicked his sentence.

Peter was going to deny such a thought, but then he realized that this man knew something and might help him. After much soul searching, Peter sat down, drew the chair near to the old man and started, slowly, to tell him the story that began that cold spring night last March.

A.E. inched closer to listen, making crunchy noises with his beak and fluffing his feathers every so often. At the end of the story, which came to a close at the Buddhist restaurant, Peter sat back waiting from a comment from the old man. He realized at that point that he did not even know the name of the old man, let alone anything about him. And yet here he was, spilling out his secrets to him.

A.E. leaned back at the end of the story and shook out his tail. He looked straight at Peter and decided to hop down to be at his side. Once he was a feather's breadth away from Peter's hand, A.E. put his head down and made little squeaky noises.

"I think he wants you to scratch his head. He must have liked the story; he usually bites anyone who ventures up into my castle."

Moving slowly, so as not to frighten the bird, Peter started to scratch the bird's head. A.E. closed his eyes and groaned with pleasure. He turned his head this way and that so that Peter could scratch just the right places. The old man started to laugh.

"You are definitely a hit. I think he is in love with you."

When Peter eventually withdrew his hands A.E. fluffed himself up and sat in a contented heaven. The old man leaned forward to Peter and looked straight into his eyes.

"So, I gather you want to know how to get into the faery realm then, without going to sleep?" Peter became excited. He had thought that any mention of the faery realm would end up with him classified as a madman. He nodded to the old man and then looked around him.

"Don't we have to go and find a forest or something?" said Peter.

The man looked at Peter blankly for a second and then started to laugh.

"Oh, Gods no, young lad. The faery realm is here, it always has been, always will be. The city is just a temporary scum on the surface of the land. Civilizations come and go; the faeries just wait for all the concrete to vanish back into the forest. It always happens; you mark my saying."

"These days, you get into the faery realm through vision, through the imagination. Your mind is like a car that carries you there. The pictures you see are from the imagination, but what you experience is real. The beings are real and are there whether you exist or not. Your mind just gives you a window through which you can talk to them. That is why they made contact with you through your sleep. But when you go in vision, it is always good to have someone from the animal world to go with you."

"That is why A.E. hangs out with me. He makes sure I don't end up in outer Bolivia or somewhere. So, are you ready, young man? If you are, close your eyes and listen to my voice."

Peter sat back and got himself comfortable, but not too comfortable. He did not want to fall asleep. He felt A.E. edge his way closer to the chair, and now that Peter had his eyes shut the power of the bird felt stronger than before.

Listening to the old man's voice was like listening to beautiful ancient music from a distant land. Peter tried to concentrate on the voice and not allow his thoughts to invade. He found himself feeling as if he were falling down through the building, down through the concrete, the sewers, then the rock, and into the earth.

Down and down they fell, and Peter was aware of A.E. flying alongside him. As they passed through the rock and earth, Peter felt as if he was being filtered and cleansed. Old stuff, emotions, poisons, and worries fell away from him as he passed through the solid rock, leaving him feeling clear and light.

He landed on top of something and he felt around to try and find out what it was. After stroking the surface, he realized it was bark. Confusion set in until he realized that it was a tree, and that he seemed to be climbing down the inside of an inverted tree.

He climbed and climbed, down and down, until he arrived at branches. Jumping out of the branches, he landed heavily on grass. A.E. plopped down behind Peter and waddled over to him. Peter sensed the old man land beside him and almost immediately he felt surrounded by many beings.

He remembered the landscape from his dreams; the grass that lit the world and the upside-down trees. The old man set off walking across the landscape and Peter ran to keep up. A.E. gave up trying to walk and flew onto Peter's shoulder, playfully pulling on Peter's ear as they went.

Peter could hear many whispers around him, but he could see nothing. Not until they came to a field full of beautiful red poppies. He wanted to lie down among them: the urge was almost painful. Peter could not resist it and A.E. jumped off his shoulder, landing among the flowers as Peter fell to his knees.

He lay down, drinking in the pleasure of the flowers as they wrapped him in a sheet of happiness and tranquility. Whispers and giggles echoed around him and he started to see shadows out of the corner of his eyes. Something moved behind him and he rolled over lazily to see what it was. He lay on his side, staring, with his mouth open.

"Shut your mouth," called out A.E. as Peter gazed upon the most beautiful woman he had ever seen. If he was ever going to fall for a woman, it would be this one.

Her eyes fixed on him and he became uncomfortable. Her eyes bored into him, searching his soul and Peter became frightened. Her eyes ripped him apart, exposing all of his deeds for her to see. Peter cried out in fear and terror. Then he saw a vision of himself crying into the chalice and his fear subsided.

She spoke. "I am the Woman of the Earth and these are my people. When they thirsted, you gave them to drink. When there was danger, you sat and kept vigil. When my children sprouted, you sang them lullabies. Peter the Bard, I give you three wishes. Guard them well."

"I wish I could see the faeries."

He blurted it out before he could stop himself and the old man groaned behind him. Peter turned around to find out what he had done wrong. The old man told him in no uncertain tones. "Fool. You have just wasted one wish. You will be able to see them anyway; they were just hiding. They wanted to see that you had a good heart before they came out of hiding."

Almost immediately hundreds and hundreds of beings of all shapes and sizes surrounded him. Some looked human, some looked like animals, some looked like flowers and trees. Some looked like things he had never seen before.

They all circled him and stared before laughing and clapping. Peter was not sure how to react. He did not know what they were laughing at. A.E. hopped over to him and looked up at him.

"They are laughing and clapping because they have just recognized you as the man who played the harp. They will want you to play for them after the meal. Will you do that?"

Peter looked at A.E. in astonishment. He was not sure what excited him most, a conversing crow or a host of faery fans.

They all tried to grab him by the sleeve, and together they led him across the grass and into a forest. They danced through the trees and in and out of the bushes, coaxing him ever deeper into the woods.

They reached a clearing where animals were seated around the periphery as if waiting for a show to start. The faery beings bounced in holding large tureens of food that seemed to have materialized from thin air. The lids of the tureens were taken off with great relish and the platters placed before the animals for approval.

The platters were piled high with fruit, berries, leaves of all different colors, apple pies, breads, and a large dish of red juice. One of the faery beings offered Peter a cup and pointed to the juice. He nodded politely and scooped his cup into the juice. The faeries all slowed down to watch and see if he would drink it. Their lips smacked and their tongues wiggled as they waited with bated breath until the cup had reached Peters lips.

The first sip tasted like wine. The second taste was like strawberries, the third was like dewdrops and the fourth was of honey. He smiled and tipped the cup back, drinking deeply with his eyes shut in pleasure. A.E. looked away and groaned.

The old man puffed into the circle, coming in last just in time to see Peter drink of the faery juice. He clapped his hands to his forehead and sighed.

"Oh, by the way, don't eat or drink in the faery realm."

The old man's feeble voice did not reach Peter who was rolling around the floor giggling like a baby; the faery beings were rolling with him, laughing. One of the faeries held out a fruit to him and Peter bit into it. A strength and vitality flowed through him causing him to jump to his feet and dance like a madman. He danced and danced until he came to a full stop before a harp.

It was the most exquisite harp he had ever seen. The wood was carved with many faces peering out around the directions and each of the faces had eyes of rubies and pearls. The harp was covered in gold leaves and the strings felt like silk.

He sat on a tree root and laid the harp to his breast. The harp seemed to move under his embrace, like a lover newly awakened. His fingers ran across the strings, emitting an unearthly sound that brought each being to a stop.

All the animals, all the faeries, the old man, and A.E. sat at

Peter's feet with their eyes turned to his hands. Peter closed his eyes. He wanted to play his favorite song, but his fingers seemed to have lost the memory. Instead, something started to push into his thoughts, something from deep down within him.

The song rose up from his heart and expressed itself through his fingers. Music of the forest spilled out of the harp and all the collected audience sighed. His fingers painted a vision of a time long gone, a time before humans started to build.

Visions of ancient trees touching the sky, flowers large enough to sleep in, a forest floor moving with life, a man child curled asleep in a tree beside a large cat. His heart sang through the harp until the song reached his lips.

In a language as old as the oldest tree, Peter sang of the brothers and sisters of the forest and the mountains. He sang of the union between underworld and overworld. He sang of love between the worlds and of children born under a peaceful sun.

Because he sang with his eyes closed, Peter did not see the ladies of the trees one by one appearing between the branches. Their hair was of leaves and their skin of bark. Eyes that seemed to hold the light of the stars looked upon Peter in wonder.

One of them tiptoed up to Peter as he sang and put a golden acorn at his feet. Another placed a green leaf at his side, and another propped a branch beside his tree root. When he had finished his song, he opened his eyes to see the audience sitting in silence, many pairs of large eyes fixed on him.

Something made him look down. He saw the golden acorn and picked it up. Before he knew what he was doing, he ate the acorn. A.E. shook his head and clicked his beak in despair.

The acorn grew inside him, bubbling up every ounce of mischief that was in his bones. His hands returned to the harp and he began to play a jig. His fingers danced across the strings as the faery beings danced with the animals.

The old man was swirled around with A.E. hopping in and out of the foray, squawking at the top of his voice. The dance got faster and faster as Peter's hands flew across the strings in frenzy. He hummed and sang along, as the feet of the faeries seemed to make the ground shake. They danced through the night until Peter felt he could play no more.

He fell asleep, still embracing the harp, which snuggled up to his warm body. A.E. was laid on his back with his legs in the air, snoring his head off with a profusion of sleeping faeries all around him.

As Peter slept, he dreamed of the surface world. He walked down the streets of Manhattan and saw for the first time the pain and fear in people's eyes. He saw the faery beings huddled around a blade of grass like street people huddling around a fire. He heard the sad songs and the weeping. He saw the poisons trickling down the street: the death, the hatred, and the anger that the people had built around themselves.

The empty nighttime streets were full of faeries forlornly sitting on steps, trashcans, and litter, their faces tired and worn from the everyday struggle of survival in a hostile world. The pain was more than he could carry. He cried out to the wind to tell him what he could do.

The wind swirled around him in answer. The answer got louder and turned into a chant that awoke him. All the faeries that had been sleeping around him sat up and joined in the chant. The ladies of the forest, the birds and the animals all joined in until it was deafening.

> *Eat of no creature, nor steal of her milk.*
> *Take of no flower not petal nor scent*
> *Drink not of liquor*
> *Nor poisons thereof*
> *And you will see faerie and nature within.*

The non-rhyming rhyme rang around his head until he thought he was going to burst. The gathered clans shouted out to him,

"Peter, do you agree to this vow, which will bind you as our brother?"

Peter nodded slowly. All of the faeries put their hands to their ears in a comic gesture. They wanted to hear the words from his own lips.

"Yes!"

He shouted the single word from the top of his voice. They all stood still and silent for a minute. Then, instruments were pulled out of jackets and from behind trees. A frenzy of wild dance music exploded out and Peter's feet took off, carrying him along in a fast energetic dance that led through the forest and back to the grass. Everyone followed, with A.E. having to fly to keep up. They emerged out of the forest and danced across the grass to the upside-down trees. The old man was already there and waiting impatiently. He kept looking at his watch, and many of the assembled faeries copied him, looking at imaginary watches on their wrists. Peter danced up to a tree and jumped up trying to catch a branch. The faeries copied, laughing as they fell over in their comic efforts.

Peter managed to grasp a low branch, hauling himself up into the tree. The faeries and animals became still and silent. One called his name and handed him the branch and leaf from the forest ladies. He put them in his pocket and started to climb.

A.E. and the old man were already climbing and Peter was half way up the tree before he realized that he was leaving the faery realm. He wanted to stop and jump back down. He did not want to go back to the surface world. But the tree that he was climbing pleaded with him to continue. "You will be our brother who watches over us, who protects the animals, birds, flowers, plants and trees. You will ensure that we will still have a world on the surface to play in."

Peter was full of sadness, but he understood that he could do things that they could not, just as they could do things that he could not. Surely, between them, they would be able to make a difference in the cold decaying world on the surface.

A.E. transferred over to Peter's tree and sat on his head as they ascended to the surface world. Peter became aware of the old man telling him to think of the room in which he first started, to remember the books and the chair upon which he was seated.

The faery realm faded away. The tree withdrew from his vision and Peter felt heaviness on his lap. He opened his eyes to find A.E. sitting there.

The old man smiled at Peter. It took Peter a while to reorient himself. The old man told Peter that now he had been there, he could find his own way back by seeing the roots of the tree in his own world and that if he climbed down the tree, he would access the faery realm.

There were many questions that Peter wanted to ask, but the old man held up his hand for silence. "No more, I'm too tired. Come back tomorrow and we will talk. Let yourself out, I'm going to sleep."

There was so much that Peter wanted to say. *Thank you* was the least of them. But he respected the old man's wishes and left, walking carefully down the steep steps. When he got out onto the street, he looked at his watch.

He looked again and tapped the glass. Only ten minutes had passed since he left the restaurant. But that was impossible! He had talked to the man for nearly an hour before doing the vision. He put his hands in his pockets and set off to walk home. His fingers played with something for a few moments before he began to realize what it was. Carefully, he pulled out a tiny leaf and a twig from his pocket. He remembered the gifts given to him in the faery realm and he stopped walking and looked at them carefully.

The leaf was much smaller than he remembered but its colors were not like the dull brown they had been in the faery realm. He turned the tiny leaf this way and that to try and count the colors that sparkled off the surface of this tiny fragment of nature.

Reds, gold, yellow, blues that were deeper than anything he could imagine flashed and changed with the dull light that was around him. The colors changed as he moved the leaf. Greens, brighter than the loudest sweater that Chris had bought him, flashed through the blue as Peter rested the leaf in his hand. Then the gust of wind came. It was too quick. The leaf blew out of his hand, and Peter was left standing on the end of 6th Avenue, his heart broken.

The following morning, Peter told Chris about his experience. Chris sat in silence with one eyebrow raised. He did not know what to make of what Peter told him. He had always known there was something unearthly about Peter and he also knew that Peter did not lie. He was a bright and honest soul, which was why Chris had fallen in love with him in the first place.

After breakfast in the Village they set out to Union Square to search out the old man. He had promised to speak with Peter today, and Peter was sure that he would not object to Chris coming along. They arrived outside the door that led to the old man's apartment. Peter knocked loudly, but no one answered. They both knocked and knocked until the door opened and a security guard emerged with a trashcan.

"Excuse me, do you know if the old man is in?" asked Peter. The security guard looked at Peter in confusion.

"What old man?"

Peter frowned and replied, "The old man who lives up there."

Peter pointed up the stairs to the attic room beyond. The security guard looked at Peter as if he was crazy.

"No old man lives up there. It's empty, and has been since, oh jeez, forever. There was an apartment up there but as far as I know it hasn't been used, not as long as I have been here anyway, and I have been here for thirty years."

Peter was beside himself. He knew it was the right place and he knew he was not crazy. "Please, I know this is a strange request, but can I go up there and look, please?"

The security guard looked at the two men. Now, he knew people, and he knew that these two weirdos did not want to do any harm. He knew that he shouldn't, but the young man looked very distressed. Maybe he was searching for a relative or something.

He nodded his head and looked up and down the street. He hoped that his judgment was not wrong, although there was nothing up there to steal.

He led the two men up the long flights of stairs to an attic room. It was empty, dusty and dirty. No one had been up there for years and Peter looked around in despair. Something caught the corner of his eye, and bending to the floor he found a crow's feather, long and black. The guard looked at the feather and then at the roof.

"They get in during the winter and warm their toes here. OK, that's it. Out you go, there is no old man here."

The guard herded them both back down the stairs and Peter fought hard to keep his emotions in check. When they got back down to the street the guard stopped Peter.

"There is someone you can ask. Two blocks down, there is a small cafe. The old woman behind the counter, Eddy, has always lived around here. If anyone would know about your Grandpa, she would."

Peter smiled through his sadness that the guard would presume he was searching for his grandpa. He thanked the guard, offering to buy him breakfast some morning, and the guy shouted back to Peter as he walked down the road that he would keep him to that promise.

Chris and Peter found the cafe with the old woman in it, and decided to stay with the idea of Grandpa. They described the attic apartment and the old man with the crow. The old lady screwed her face up in thought. She was sixty-nine, but remembered from when she was seven years old her mother telling her about an old man and a crow that she used to bake bread for.

Peter guided the old woman to a table and sat her down with a cup of tea. The old woman shouted to her assistant to take over while she had a break and Peter tried hard to focus the woman without pushing her.

"Please tell us what you remember, it's very important to me."

The old woman frowned suspiciously at Peter and Chris. But there was something in Peter's eyes that told her she should help him.

"I remember my mother baking bread every Tuesday for the old man. He would have no milk or egg in the bread, which made it very hard to bake. I never did learn what she put in it, but she made it for me when I was little and it always tasted good. She used to tell me that the bread would help me see faeries.

"There was also a crow that the old man cared for and his place was full of books. Everywhere you looked it was books. I think the owner of the building let him live there for free. Now this was back in the thirties, mind you. But she started looking after him in the twenties before I came along. I think she said he was an Irish poet and writer but I cannot remember his name.

"So that was your grandfather. Well, looking at you he must

be your great-grandfather." Peter nodded excitedly. This was the same man.

As they left the cafe, Peter's happiness wore off. Although he had found the man and proved to Chris that what he had said was true, that he was not crazy, he had lost his connection to the faery realm. The weight of it bore down on him as they walked home.

It was not until he got on to the portion of West 19th street, between 8th and 9th Ave, the stretch of road where he lived, that he saw the weeds poking out of the ground. It was then that he remembered the old man's words,

"See the roots of the tree in the surface world and climb down the tree. There you find the faery realm."

CHAPTER 2

A TALE OF STONES

A damp wind blew incessantly around the stones as Hillary, for the fourteenth time, circled them in curiosity. She had saved her hard-earned dollars for three years and flown across the Atlantic from America, just so that she could stand here among the ancient stones of Beigh moor.

The anticlimax almost drove her to tears. The stones seemed dead, lifeless in the face of her enthusiasm, as she went from stone to stone, touching them with her forehead. Nothing.

A lone bird flew overhead, calling to her in her stupidity. This was the third day that she had ventured out of Cookstown to stand in the peat bog and marvel at the ancient stone alignments. Rain dripped off the edge of her chin, taking all her hopes and longings with it as it fell to the ground, leaving her with nothing. What had she expected?

For years she had read books about Celtic stone circles, Celtic history, Celtic myths. The blood of her father's family pulled at her to discover Ireland for herself, to walk the paths that her ancestors had frequented. But now that she was here, the rain and smell of damp peat was the only thing that had impressed itself on her.

Driving back into the town, she nodded to the old man sitting outside the pub. He was always there, regardless of the weather. Hillary came to the conclusion that he never went home, but lived on the wet bench under the Guinness sign. He smiled as she drove past and Hillary cringed. She was convinced that the whole town was laughing at her, the American who sits in the rain staring at stones.

The following morning, her last day in Cookstown, the sun graced the world with its presence and shone down upon the stones at Beigh moor. Hillary, as always, went to the stones straight after breakfast. She parked her car and carried a blanket through the wet grass to the assemblage of stone circles half buried in the peat.

Standing to catch her breath, she covered her eyes from the sun and looked around the moor. In the mist and rain, she had not been able to see much. But now, in the sunshine, the vastness of the stone alignments became frightening clear to her. They went on for miles, mostly hidden except for the very tips of the stones that peeked out of the wet peat.

The heavy blanket proved to be a good barrier against the damp as she sat in the center of the largest circle and began to sketch the alignments. The curlews called to her as she sat in the weak sunshine trying to absorb as much as she could from this magical place before the long flight home.

Shielding her eyes from the sun, Hillary squinted as she systematically looked at the alignments in sections. Not only did she want to draw them, but she also wanted to fix their appearance in her mind forever. There were three apparent circles, with the stones half buried in the bog. Beside the circles stood small collapsed cairns that served well as perches. Hillary had been tempted to sit on one rather than on the grass. But as she had approached the collapsed pile of stones, some instinct warned her off. "What if was a grave?" she asked herself.

Beyond the clear circles stretching out into the peat bog were numerous stones that lay half hidden beneath mud and grass. She was tempted to follow the stones and explore just how far the alignments stretch. But the voice of the local pub owner emerged in her head. She had popped into the local pub the night before for a Guinness and the barman had asked her why on earth she was in Cookstown.

When she told him she was here to visit the stones, he had roared with laughter. When the laughter had finished, his face grew serious. "Don't you be going beyond the circles now, do yer hear? Strange things happen out there and people vanish. Now you mind yerself and take care." Hillary smiled, but fear slid into her previously confident thoughts and she nodded quietly.

Tipping her head back to drink her Guinness, she caught the old men in the pub looking at her and shaking their heads sadly. As each man got up to go home to his meal and his wife, they first stopped by Hillary as she sat at the bar, and patted her shoulder solemnly while shaking their heads.

Now, as she sat drinking in the stones, she did not feel any danger or fear. Taking their advice, she had not wandered off, but remained within the circle that drew her most: the larger one at the far end of the alignment on the edge of the bog.

After only a short time, her head became heavy and her eyes struggled to stay open. She had only been awake a few hours, yet Hillary had to fight a sleepiness that crept upon her, threatening to take away her precious last few hours with the stones. Rubbing her eyes, she began to sing to keep herself awake. Rabbits darted past and something, perhaps shadows in the low sunshine, moved around the edge of her vision as though watching her.

The battle waged until finally, Hillary closed her eyes and

lay back in the damp warmth. The sketches danced around the stones, carried by a strange wind that only blew around the alignments. Hillary did not notice as she fell deeper and deeper into a dark sleep. The wind grew stronger, pulling at her hair as though to tease her and whispering a song in payment for Hillary's song.

The sound of the song carried only to the edge of the stone circle and no further. Beyond the stones, all was stillness and calm. The song pulled Hillary from the depth of her sleep, keeping her on the edge of awareness, but not allowing her to open her eyes. She struggled, while trapped in her half sleep, to hear the words that carried around the stones.

> *Ring stone round, ring stone round,*
> *Bring rain and wind and thunder sound,*
> *Storms will dance while you do tarry*
> *And only stones your heart will marry*
> *Whatever shall it be, whatever shall it be...*

Hillary drifted on the threshold of sleep. "Whatever shall it be. The words circled around her head, digging for memories. Quite suddenly, without warning, Hillary was transported back through time into a memory of her childhood in California. At only eight years old, she stood on top of a hill near her hometown of Petaluma and held her arms up to the sky.

Hillary remembered the taste of the memory. She was playing on the top of upside-down hill, her name for a towering hill where water was fabled to run uphill and where lanes vanished to confuse the drivers. Something had stopped her game of tag with the butterflies and caused her to stare into nothing. A rush of power formed a wind that blew only where Hillary stood and the little girl held her arms up to the sky in wonder.

In that second, Hillary saw a terrible storm with flooding

and mudslides. She watched as her grandmother's house, on a steep hill by Tomales Bay, slid into the water with Grandmother trapped inside it. In terror, Hillary screamed out for her grandmother and looked up to shout at the storm.

The powerful being that was the storm looked down in anger at Hillary: its rage centered on the humans who had desecrated sacred power lands. Suddenly the wind ceased and the vision faded, leaving the little girl shaking and crying on top of upside-down hill.

Hillary jerked awake, finding herself back on the damp blanket on Beigh moor. She lay for a second trying to orientate herself. The dream of her childhood had been very vivid, and she had forgotten about that incident until now. The wind had stopped but her drawings were scattered all over the circles. It had left a strange scent in the air, a scent that she could almost taste: and a scent that she remembered from that childhood day on upside-down hill.

Hillary sat up, pulling her knees under her arms and placing her chin on her knees—her thinking position, particularly when something frightened her. The storm she had seen in that vision as a child happened two weeks later. She had told her grandmother about the vision, which had caused her mother to react angrily towards Hillary. Hillary's grandmother and mother argued for hours while Hillary lay outside on the lawn weeping. She always seemed to cause trouble and she hated that. It was not as though she did it on purpose.

Two weeks after, when a storm whipped up and began moving into the bay, grandmother put the cats in the car and headed inland to her daughter's house, just to be on the safe side. The house did slide down into the bay but Hillary was not allowed to talk about it.

The day after, when her mother returned with the grandmother to what was left of the house, Hillary's mother had spun around and pointed a finger into Hillary's face. "Don't you ever speak of this to anyone, do you hear me? Not ever. You saw nothing and said nothing." Hillary nodded dumbly, unable to understand what she had done wrong. Had she not saved grandmother's life?

Some of the residue pain from that time bubbled up in Hillary's eyes. Her mother had been distant with her from that moment. Her father was always away and only Grandmother seemed thankful for what Hillary had seen. Now, as a mature woman, she sat and wept for her mother and her lost child-hood. All because of a strange day and a strange wind.

Slowly, she got up and started to pick up the drawings that were scattered untidily around the stones. But each time she reached out for one, a breeze picked it up and moved it. She chased the pictures around the circle until the breeze turned into a wind, carrying the drawings high up into the air before dropping them just out of her reach.

A laugh echoed from behind her and Hillary spun around to see an old man and his large black dog leaning against one of the stones. "I see they like you. Wind is good; they have woken up. About time too, I should say." His accent was deep and broad, causing Hillary to look blank as she tried to figure out what he just said.

"What do you mean, they have woken up?" Hillary was excited, but she tried very hard not to show it. The old man waved a hand around the stones as he spoke. "This lot. When the wind blows here and nowhere else, it means they are prepared to work with whoever is in the circle. It's easy. Just walk around the circle until you are fit to drop and then go sit in the middle. They will show you the rest. Have to go, my dinner's getting cold."

The wind blew Hillary's hair across her face and it took her a second or two to get the hair out of her eyes. She cleared her face and looked around, but the man had vanished. Hillary turned in all directions. It was impossible to vanish so quickly;

the moor was flat for miles and there was nowhere to vanish *to*. She should have been able to see him walk away for a least a mile in any direction. But he was nowhere to be seen. The hairs on the back of her neck stood up to attention in terror.

Her hands fumbled for the scattered pictures as her eyes kept watch for the disappearing man. Hillary was frightened and excited all at once. She had read about such encounters in her Celtic books. Of course! She slapped her forehead in recognition of her stupidity. The legend of the guardian with the black dog: the guardian of the stones. She must have read about such apparitions a hundred times, and when it happened to her, she did not recognize him.

There would have been so many things she could have asked him, so many things she could have learned. Swearing under her breath, she caught the last picture and weighed them down with a stone. What an idiot, she thought to herself. And yet, did he not tell her something? Her mind filtered through the details of the conversation until she remembered what it was that he had said.

"Circle the stones until you are fit to drop. Then sit down and let them do the rest."

Hillary looked around her, just to make sure there was no one to watch what she was doing. When she was sure that she was alone, Hillary began to walk clockwise around the stones. She had chosen the biggest circle, which was surrounded by small Cairns. Around and around she circled, trying hard to concentrate on what she was doing.

An hour passed and Hillary's legs were beginning to hurt. She had given up concentrating, and instead, amused herself by mulling over her life in America. She had looked into the possibility of moving to Ireland and she had been excited to find that she would be able to get an Irish passport on the strength of her grandfather's birth in Cork. Maybe she would move to Cookstown and live on the edge of the bog. Then she would never have to leave the stones. Reality came crashing back with her footfalls when she admitted to herself that she could not afford to move and that there was no way for her to make a living out here in the middle of nowhere.

The resentment at her trapped life caused Hillary to walk faster. Why did life always do this to her? Why did things never work out? Why did she always lose things when she loved them? Her heart ached for permanence and love: she needed to belong and be loved. Unhappiness punctured every footfall as she marched around the circle deep in thought.

Her legs started to tremble from the unaccustomed exercise, but Hillary pushed on, circling and circling as she thought of her life in Manhattan, the city where she had settled after college. Everything was fast, young, successful, and unhappy. Manhattan had hidden her from herself, allowing her to function in the world of frenzy. But here, among the stones and birds, Hillary could not hide.

It was the knees that buckled first. The pain shot through both knees bringing Hillary to an abrupt halt. She walked gingerly into the center and lay down upon the damp, rough moor grass. Exhausted, she allowed her body to slump as she lay watching the clouds scurry past on an intent mission to rain upon some poor unsuspecting soul. Her body lapped up the rest, and her skin soaked up the moisture from the damp air as she lay in wait for what was to come.

But nothing happened. She lay waiting patiently, not knowing what to expect. The minutes moved on and Hillary was beginning to feel stupid. Maybe she had imagined the old man. Maybe she had dreamt him? Her body was too tired to care and Hillary drifted slowly to sleep, serenaded by the birds and the light wind.

Just as she tipped over the edge of sleep, her mind plummeted down at high speed through the land. The rush terrified her as she fought to awaken, but something held her firmly in the grip of unconsciousness. A whirlwind ripped at her as she fell, twisting and turning her until she could neither feel nor see anything except wind. At that point, the wind ceased but the falling continued. She looked down and saw the earth, the planet beneath her, and she was falling towards it at high speed.

Hillary tried to cry out, but nothing would move. The planet was getting closer and closer as she tried to pull away from the imminent impact. Breath froze in her throat as the ground rushed up to her face and Hillary closed her eyes in horror. There was no impact: everything was still, and Hillary lay on the grass with her eyes still shut. She opened them slowly, sitting up so that she could look around her.

The damp blanket was still there, but everything else was different: the stones had gone and bright lights had replaced them. Hillary sat unmoving as the lights pulsated brilliant colors that seemed to seep up into the sky and join with the sun. In among the lights where the stones had been, Hillary could see people, almost shadows, moving between the lights. The people appeared briefly before vanishing, their place then taken by another human shadow that moved as though unaware of its predecessor.

Some moved randomly and others seemed to be conducting a ritual. Hillary watched in awe. Something, maybe instinct, told her that she was seeing through time: the shadows were people who had visited and worked with the stones over the centuries. Moving very slowly, Hillary tried to approach one of the lights which, she now understood, were the stones. As her hand reached out and touched the light, a shadow moved swiftly around her. Her hand felt the cold stone but all she could see was light and movement. Her eyes focused on the movement of the shadow, which transformed into the hazy image of a child. The child could see Hillary and was frightened.

Hillary held her hand up to the child to tell her not to be afraid, but as she removed her hand from the stone the child vanished, leaving only the bright light to blind her. This fascinated her. She touched the stone again, feeling its solidness through the light as its power coursed through her. Again, she saw shadows move around her. A shadow approached the stone that Hillary was touching. As the shadow touched the stone, Hilary could see it was a young man. She touched him on the forehead and the young man jumped back in terror, his face contorting as he clutched his head. She panicked. What if she had injured him?

She touched the stone again, this time closing her eyes from the distractions around her. As soon as her lids shut, the ground started to spin beneath her. Hillary felt nauseous but refused to let go of the stone. The spinning became faster and faster until the sensation became comfortable: Hillary understood that she was now going at the same speed as the stone. She opened her eyes and looked up. Weather fronts passed and vanished. Night and day moved rapidly and the wind came and went.

She leaned back into the stone, which supported her as she looked up. The deeper into the stone she leaned, the clearer her vision became. As the storm fronts passed over, Hillary became aware that they were beings; that the storms had consciousness. She reached up towards one as it passed over, her mind searching for contact.

Immediately she was traveling with the storm as it passed over the land and sea. Its fury built within her as it sought to cleanse the land with its power. The rain was unleashed on the land and Hillary fell with the raindrops, touching everything around her and sensing the consciousness scattered in every drop of water.

The land breathed in response to the storm, creating a conversation that had Hillary in the middle. The land and the storm communed, and Hillary joined in. Her body felt the interaction, lapping up the life-giving water and enjoying the feel of release as the land gave power to the storm.

It stopped as suddenly as it had started and Hillary was back, leaning against the stone. Her body felt heavy from the exertion and she slumped harder against the standing stone, which seemed to absorb her. The feeling of absorption became more intense until Hillary slipped into the stone and became one with the rock.

Her breathing slowed, her thoughts deepened, and her movements ceased as she joined in union with the sacred stone. All the other stones in the circle connected with her, communing in their vigil on the power site. Each stone was a combination of priest or priestess, and rock. Hillary took her place as priestess of the land and became one with the stone.

The cycles of the earth came and went as the seasons passed over her. Her thoughts guided those who wished to commune with the sacred land and her joy was immeasurable as the power of the Underworld flowed through her reaching for the sky, while the power of the stars flowed down through her on its way into the Underworld. This was what she was born for; this was the purpose of her existence.

The breath came suddenly, and a dull light crashed into Hillary's brain. Voices echoed all around her as someone called her name. She felt her body being moved and sharp needle pricks in her wrist. Hillary tried to open her eyes. A voice shouted in her face, its noise deafening in its coarseness. "Can you hear me, miss? Miss, can you hear me?"

Hillary tried to turn away from the noise as she sought the peaceful stillness of the stones. But she could not move her head. Reluctantly, she slowly opened her eyes, and looked at a face peering into hers. Everything was dull: the sky, the face peering over her and the people around her. Nothing had light or color. Hillary wanted to die. The face spoke to her again as she tried to focus on the intruder.

"We are going to put you in the ambulance now, everything is going to be OK. It was a good piece of luck that Mr. Henry found you, eh?"

Hillary did not want putting into an ambulance; she wanted to be left with the stones. As they carried her out of the circle, Hillary felt the stones pull on her to stay. But there was nothing she could do but cry as she was driven off away from where she belonged.

THE MALE NURSE bustled around her as Hillary stared out of the window. After a battery of tests over many days, they had finally agreed to let her go. Words like epilepsy and drugs had been bandied about among the doctors, which had made Hillary very angry. And yet she could offer no alternative explanation without exposing the secrets of the stones.

The male nurse watched Hillary closely as she packed her bags. He looked towards the door and then back at Hillary. He spoke to her in a low voice, keeping one eye on the door and one on Hillary. "Miss, my name is Fra. I was born near Beigh moor. It's a very special place, isn't it?" He waited for Hillary's reaction. She sat down and looked at him more closely. There was something in his eyes that she had not noticed previously, a brilliant fragment of light.

She nodded slowly in response to his comment. "Did you work with the stones then? Is that why you were there?" He turned as he asked her the questions, making sure that no one could see him from the corridor. Hillary nodded and Fra watched the nod in the room mirror.

"Well," he continued, "If you want to work with them properly, there are ways of doing it without killing yourself. Call me and my granddad will teach you." Fra shoved a piece of torn paper into Hillary's hand and then darted down the corridor and out of sight before she could speak to him.

She fingered the paper in her hand and looked back at her bag that contained her air ticket. Hillary reached into her bag and pulled out the wallet that held her passport and plane ticket. Without a second thought, she tore the ticket into bits and threw them into the bin. The sky darkened, lowering the light in the room and Hillary got up to look out of the window. Clouds were gathering: she could feel the power of the storm as it edged nearer, calling on her to join it.

She slung her bag over her shoulder and picked up her suitcase, which had been dropped off by her hotel. On the threshold of the hospital, she looked again at the sky and breathed its scent as she stepped out into a new world. There would be no going back now.

CHAPTER 3
THE FINGERS OF ANGELS

PART ONE

Peggy grabbed the toast as she ran to the door, one eye on the clock and one eye on the shoe that refused to go onto her foot unaided. She pushed and shoved her foot, cursing through the mouthful of bread as the shoe danced around the carpet, avoiding her squirming foot.

Lizzy slurped her porridge and laughed at Peg, who was trying to curse without her mother hearing her. Finally, the shoe gave in and stayed still long enough for Peg to ease her foot into the high heeled torture instrument and totter off with her bag over one shoulder, her hat half on and her other arm half into her coat.

"Bye, love! Have a good day at school," called Peg's mother as Peg vanished into the dark winter morning. Her black regulation school coat soon ensured that Peg became invisible and her white rabbit fur hat stood out alone, bobbing down the path as she ran.

Lizzy savored the last mouthful of oats mingled with treacle before staring at the pile of books that were ready and waiting for her on the hallway table. She was about to get up and put her coat on when the room fell away from her. Her eyes glazed over and Peg walked past her vision into the path of an oncoming motorbike. The bike hit Peg with such force that she was tossed into the air like a tennis ball.

Lizzy let out a horrific scream and fell to her knees. Her mother ran in and grabbed hold of her, trying to ascertain what was wrong with her. All Lizzy could see was Peg's white rabbit fur hat laying in the center of the road. Through her sobbing, she told her mother that a motorbike had hit Peg.

"Oh, please, Lizzy, you have to stop this silliness. You could not possibly see if that had happened. The path goes round the corner before you get to the road, you could not have seen such a thing. Now I have had enough of these amateur dramatics from you, young lady. You are going to school whether you like it or not, right now! So get your shoes on or you will miss the bus."

Lizzy pleaded with her mother to listen, but her mother simply propelled her into the hallway and stood with her hands on her hips as Lizzy put on her shoes while still sobbing. No one ever listened to her. She was ten years old now and still no one ever listened to her.

She was just about to put her coat on when someone approached the front door. The figure of a tall man loomed through the glass door, and just as she called her mother back out of the kitchen, the doorbell rang. Lizzy`s heart sank as deep as the coalmines. She knew this man was here about Peg and the accident.

Her mother scurried back out of the kitchen, desperately trying to entangle herself from her apron. She tidied her hair and then opened the door. Lizzy stood in the corner with her hands over her ears. She did not want to hear what was coming: that her beloved sister was in a pool of blood in the middle of the road.

Peg was everything that Lizzy worshiped. She was clever and witty, she could draw pictures that Lizzy could not, she always had a crowd of boys hanging around with her and she had a full set of felt tip pens that had all the lids and they all worked.

Her mother cried out as the man asked to use the telephone. He said that a little girl had just been knocked over and this was the nearest house with a telephone. Lizzy began to sob again and her mother pointed to the phone before pushing past the man and running around the corner to the main road.

She tripped on something that brought her to her knees. She looked back at her feet as she cried out in pain from the scrape of her knee to find her feet entangled in Peg's white rabbit fur hat. Grabbing the hat, she ran to the crowd that had formed on the center divide of the road and pushed herself through the gathered people to find Peg laying unconscious with a policeman trying to resuscitate her.

PART TWO

Peg dashed down the path, around the corner, and paused on the verge of the road. Her eyes darted back and forth, straining to see in the early morning darkness as the headlights dazzled and then vanished. The road seemed empty for a second, so Peg stepped out, focusing on the bus stop at the other side of the road. Was he there? Was the boy who had driven her to writing his name all over her jotter waiting for her at the bus stop? She thought she saw his outline waving frantically at her and Peg waved back, trying not to look ungainly as she tried to run in her high heels.

The impact took her breath, blinding her with a terrible brightness that tore into her brain. She felt herself travel through the air with a lightness and slowness that consumed her every thought. It seemed to go on forever. The sound of screeching brakes and crunching metal filled her world as she sailed through the air in confusion. Her body relaxed instinctively so that when she finally hit the tarmac, she bounced.

The road surface tore at her legs, scraping the skin back to expose the red flesh underneath. She heard the snap of bones before she felt the pain, which was immediately replaced by fear. Her body lay facing the oncoming traffic and the headlights screamed at her to run. She knew that if she did not move, she would die.

Somewhere, some power mingled with her fear and pain, giving her the strength to raise herself up on to her knees. Cars screamed around her, skidding with their horns blaring as they spotted her at the last minute. Nothing on her reflected light. The white rabbit hat lay covered in blood some feet away and the shouts of the children at the bus stop were drowned by the noise of the two lanes of traffic.

She must make it to the center aisle, the grass strip that divided the road. That was all that was in her world. That thin green line. Slowly, she pulled her legs under herself in an attempt to crawl an inch at a time towards the grass. She could only see from one eye and the darkness of the other eye beckoned her to lie still and sleep. But the determination to live grew strong as she hauled herself by her arms, dragging her body behind her as she went. The grass was close enough for her to smell and her arm reached out to grasp it as she hauled herself towards it.

At that instant, something hit her ankles, sending spasms of new pain into her body to join with the already growing chorus of agony that assaulted her mind and body. The car had not seen her in time to avoid hitting her.

The driver was concentrating on the chaos in front of him and did not think to look at the road surface. He felt the car go over something and it was only when his brakes brought him to a stop and he saw the body laying half in the road and half on the grass verge that he screamed out. With his hazards blaring, he left the car, ignoring the chaos of jumbled and crumpled cars ahead, and ran back to the seemingly lifeless body that lay partly on the grass.

As he got closer, he saw that the body was a woman, maybe even a girl; it was too hard to tell. He bent over as he heard someone screaming for an ambulance. Someone rushed past him, shouting that they were going to a phone. He took off his coat and laid it around the girl's body in an attempt to shut out the winter frost.

Was she breathing? He could not tell. But as the horror of the possibility of death rose to his throat, the girl groaned. He dared not move her, her injuries seemed too severe, and she was laid on her stomach, which made it hard to see anything.

He talked to the girl, telling her that everything was OK and that help was on its way. The groaning got louder and her breathing sounded bubbly. Now that he had a chance to calmly look at the girl, he recognized her grammar school uniform. He guessed that she must be all of fourteen and his heart sank as low as it could go.

He had just dropped his own daughter safely at a bus stop on his way to work. What would he do if this happened to her? His heart turned and turned, making him nauseous as he tried to block such thoughts from his head. The word of thanks went out to God as he heard the ambulance arriving. He had not accompanied his wife to church in a long time, but if this poor girl survived, he promised he would return. As soon as he uttered that promise, he felt its strength course though him and he knew that he would have to honor that promise.

PART THREE

Lizzy and her mother piled into the police car and Lizzy clung to her mother sobbing as the car followed the ambulance to the hospital.

"Why are they going so slow? Why don't they just speed like they normally do? Why are they not hurrying for my child? Please radio them and tell them to go faster."

The policeman in the passenger seat turned to face the distraught mother in the back of the car. He hated this part of the job, seeing innocent people suffer.

"I'm sorry, madam, the chances are they have to go slow because they are attending to your daughter and need a steady hand. She will get there soon enough, it's not far now."

The policeman's voice did nothing to soothe Mrs. Connor as she stared at the ambulance in front that carried her precious daughter. Her hands twisted around and around the blanket that the policeman had wrapped around her shoulders before putting her in the car. Lizzy placed her hands on her mother's hands to still them while looking up at her mother's distraught face.

"She will be OK, Mummy, I can feel it, and she will be fine."

Mrs. Connor looked through her tears to her youngest daughter and smiled. Lizzy was always full of fancy ideas, and her mother was not about to pour the water of truth over her daughter's fire of fantasy. She knew that Lizzy worshipped Peg and that this was her way of dealing with it. She blocked out the memory of what Lizzy had said about Peg before the man came to the door. Her mother, Lizzy's grandmother, had the second sight, and it had brought her nothing but misery. She was not going to let that happen to her daughter.

She had seen the state of Peg as the ambulance man had turned her ready to prepare her for transit. It would indeed take a miracle for her daughter to survive the injuries that the motorbike and car had inflicted on her thin pubescent body. Her hand played with the rosary beads as she prayed silently to the Blessed Virgin Mary to save her daughter's life.

In the hospital, the medical team did a swift assessment of the young girl's injuries. Her pelvis was shattered by the impact, right leg compound fracture, left foot dislocated and compound at the ankle, internal injuries, broken ribs, collar bone, cheek bones, eye detached on left side, three simple skull fractures, left ear severed. The internal bleeding had been brought under control by emergency surgery, but the young girl was in a deep coma and was not responding to any stimuli.

The list was read in a quiet voice to Mrs. Connor as she requested a full briefing on her child's condition. She listened silently without comment. The staff nurse put her arm around Mrs. Connor. All the emergency team knew her well. Mrs. Connor was the duty midwife for the surrounding area. She looked through the window into the intensive care unit ward that held a very still and silent Peg. Now was the time to make decisions. But she needed some time to think clearly.

Lizzy stood quietly at her side, not taking her eyes off Peg as she watched her elder sister's chest rise and fall with the life support machine. She knew that there was something she had to do for Peg, but she was not sure what it was. One thing that she did know though, was that she had to be at Peg's side.

"Can I sit with Peg for a while, please? I will pray for her and keep her company."

Lizzy tugged at her mother's dress as she pleaded to be with her sister. Lizzy`s mother looked down at her face and was about to refuse when she asked herself what the harm would be. The machines had stabilized Peg; it was just a matter of what to do next. It would probably do Lizzy good to feel that she was partaking of the situation, so her mother slowly nodded and the head staff nurse agreed.

The child stood attentive as the staff nurse reeled off a long list of dos and don'ts to Lizzy who had to agree to leave the room immediately when asked to, without question. She nodded to her mother before slipping into the room and finding a chair to pull up to the side of the bed.

The room was still; the only sounds came from the hiss and click of the life support machine as it breathed for Peg. Little lights flashed with regular beats, and screens displayed wavy lines as Peg's heart struggled to cope with the sudden burden of massive injuries. The young girl's face and body was bloated beyond its normal size and Lizzy stared in fascination. She placed her hand carefully on the bed, just in reach of Peg's, so that they touched in a gentle, fragile sense.

Almost immediately Lizzy became very tired. It had been a terrible day of panic and waiting. She had watched the door of the operating theater for four and a half hours while emergency surgery was carried out on Peg. No one had been able to get her to move until the doctor came out to say that Peg was over the first hurdle but had slipped into a deep coma.

Slowly, Lizzy's eyes shut and she allowed her head to sag onto the arm of the soft chair, still keeping her hand near Peg's, just in case. The sensation of falling rushed around her and she called out Peg's name in her mind, but no one answered. She called and called until she found herself standing at the side of the bed looking at Peg. She knew she was dreaming, but she did not want to break the spell of the dream. Peg lay in a heap on the bed, her body broken and torn with a dim light shining out from it.

A large hole appeared in the ground and Lizzy peered down it. At the bottom shone a light. The light was swaying like a signal for her, and she shouted down that she had no way to get down. A voice shouted back for her to just jump, and that they would catch her. The thought that they would not never crossed Lizzy`s mind as she jumped.

The wind rushed past her as she descended down into the underworld. She fell and fell until the light of the hospital fell away, leaving her to fall through darkness. The scent of fresh earth swirled around her as she fell, passing through tree roots, rocks, caverns and springs until finally, they too fell away, and she tumbled through nothing. The lights below got nearer and nearer, and she started to slow down.

Each light got brighter and brighter until they began to hurt Lizzy`s eyes. She placed her arms up over her eyes to protect them and in doing so, did not see what was coming next.

The lights seemed to travel away from her and the sensation of falling down a well ended abruptly as she fell out of the earth and tumbled out into the stars. The speed of her fall slowed down to nearly a stop. She gazed around in wonder.

Lizzy was slowly moving through the stars, drifting in silence. She stretched out in the silence, enjoying the dream and drinking in the regenerating power of the stars. Somewhere, a noise broke through the stillness. It sounded like a rushing of air and a horn sounding all at once.

The noise got louder and louder until it started to push into Lizzy`s brain. The pressure pushed against her as the sound blasted through the heavens and Lizzy thought she was going to explode. Each hair on her head stood to attention, and her teeth vibrated at incredible speed, sending the waves of vibration through her body.

She became very frightened and started to call for her mother. The call vanished into the sound and returned to brush past her face. Her hair began to swarm around her as a wind from the beating of wings flowed past her. She closed her eyes in fear, sobbing for her mother in a loud voice and throwing her arms across her face in an attempt to protect herself. The beating of wings grew stronger and stronger until suddenly, there was silence. The air was still and nothing moved. Lizzy slowly moved her hands from her face and opened her eyes.

A terrible fear gripped her as she found herself surrounded by a host of angels. Each being was so tall that they looked down on Lizzy as if she were an ant. Their long silken hair streamed off into the Void, their wings outstretched, inter-linking with each other to form a circle around Lizzy, who stood terrified in the center. Each of their bodies seemed to have layers of moving color within them.

Lizzy looked closer to find that each angel was made up of many other much smaller angels. Just as she saw that, one of the angels split into hundreds of smaller ones and they all swarmed around her like bees.

One particular one moved behind her and placed his hands on her back. The moment his hands touched Lizzy she felt a shock wave of power flow through her as though she had been struck by lightning. The shock caused her to fall, and the angel fell with her, passing through the stars at a terrible speed. Lizzy tried to catch her breath as she fell, her hands frantically searching to grasp the angel in an attempt to feel safe.

Down below her, the planet rose to meet them at high speed and Lizzy thought she was going to die. She tried to remember her prayers and cried out for her mother in breath-less bursts as they plummeted towards the ever-growing planet. The angel heard her prayers and felt Lizzy's fear. He smiled through the falling and slowly, carefully, placed his wings around Lizzy until she was completely enveloped within him.

Lizzy relaxed into the warmth and safety of the wings as they fell. She allowed her body to sag against the body of the angel until they fell as one being through time and space. She felt the earth get closer; the closeness of the angel seemed to heighten her senses and she felt the despair and fear rising up to greet them as they fell. She questioned, in her mind, what it was that she was feeling and the angel answered:

"Child, behold the despair of life and the fear of death."

Lizzy wanted to squirm against the feelings and run away. But the angel held on tight as they fell ever closer to the surface of the planet. The feelings got stronger and stronger until it was almost unbearable for Lizzy. At that point, she felt them both hit something at high speed and Lizzy opened her eyes to find them both plunging through a building.

They passed through the roof of a building and through the many floors without causing damage or even a whisper of sound. They arrived in a hospital room where the angel untangled Lizzy from his wings and placed his hand on her head to steady her after the fall.

He held her for a moment while she tried to orientate herself. It was not until that moment that she realized she was in Peg's hospital room and that the sleeping child beside Peg was herself. She looked to the angel in shock. The angel merely looked at Peg and indicated to Lizzy that he wanted her to go and stand by Peg's head, behind the bed. She looked at the wall that the bed was backed up against, and looked back at the angel. The angel looked up at the ceiling that they had just passed through and Lizzy got the message.

She went and stood at the head of Peg's bed, her body half in and half out of the wall. It felt strange and yet totally natural all at the same time. The angel moved to stand behind Lizzy, placing his hands on her shoulders. He put back his head, mumbled a few words and then opened his mouth wide. A cry rang out through all the worlds as the angel passed his arms through Lizzy's arms until Lizzy and angel were truly as one.

Lizzy's body lurched with the impact. Even her sleeping body lurched, as it lay empty at the side of the bed, curled up in waiting. She felt the angel pass into her and Lizzy marveled at the power that flowed through her.

The room became transparent, and Lizzy could see through all the many rooms at once. She could see into the hearts of each and every person in the building, all at once. She could feel the power and light within the building fabric. And then she tried to turn away from a terrible whispering cry that seemed to seep around the building. It was not in Peg's room, but it seemed to be in just about every other room. Lizzy questioned what it was and the angel within her opened his heart wider so that she might see.

Each room had a vase of cut flowers and the noise was coming from them. It was at that point that Lizzy realized she was hearing the death cries of the flowers mingling with the suffering of the humans. It was about to distract her when the angel pulled her focus back to her big sister. He told her to place her hands on Peg's head, which she did. Nothing happened for a second and then, through her fingers, she began to see into Peg's body. The young girl's body was made up of a glowing, intricately woven web pattern that had been torn and damaged. Lizzy was not sure what to do. The angel reminded her of the crocheting that her mother had taught her.

Immediately a crochet needle appeared in her hands and Lizzy set about repairing the broken pattern. Her fingers worked at high speed as the angel worked through her, lending his power and skill to the dexterity and substance of Lizzy. Together they labored, delicately linking broken threads, re-attaching detached connections and creating new patterns where the old were beyond repair.

Limb by limb, the pair worked, until they reached the center of Peg's body. In the center sat an orb that glowed dimly. Its dimness worried Lizzy and the angel passed into her the knowledge of the breath of life. Lizzy felt as though she was being pumped up like a tire. She got bigger and bigger, until she began to choke as she held back the air in her body.

When she could bear it no more, she bent over her sister and breathed into the orb. Words whispered all around her, words passed through her and into Peg, and words imprinted themselves on Lizzy's heart.

The breath of life, the word, passed into the orb, which began to glow brightly. The bright golden light spilled out of the orb, passing at great speed down the web pattern, lighting the threads as it went. The light passed into Peg's hair, and then spilled out into the immediate space that surrounded her.

Lizzy felt a great urgency to contain the light and she hurriedly worked to create a boundary beyond which the light could not go. Her hands and mind worked hard building a cocoon that Peg would rest in and when the cocoon was finished, it contained the light which began to build up to a dazzling strength.

The angel and Lizzy waited for a while as Peg bathed in the bright light. Lizzy knew that something else was to be done, but she was not sure what. The angel was still and silent within her while Lizzy rested. After what seemed like an eternity to Lizzy, the angel motioned that he wanted them to move around to Peg's side.

Lizzy moved slowly. Her feet felt like they had lead boots on as she tried to walk to Peg's side. The brightness had calmed down enough for Lizzy to see into Peg. She could see that the pattern had been transformed, but her organs and limbs were still broken. She thought that she had just mended them, and Lizzy became confused. The angel responded to Lizzy, speaking through Lizzy's own thoughts.

"Her soul and pattern that allows existence has been healed from its trauma. The accident was merely a symptom of her trauma, not the cause of it. Now you must heal the shell that carries the soul, for it sustained terrible damage."

Lizzy did not understand what the angel was telling her. The angel tried hard to search within the child's mind to reach a place of wisdom so that he could show her what was happening. It was important that she understood what it was that she was doing, so that she could carry out service to her generation in times to come.

He found pictures that he could use. He showed her a sad person weeping. He showed her the weeping person getting into a car. He showed the weeping person driving and crying.

The person could not see properly because they were crying, and the car crashed. First, they had to mend the person, and then they had to mend the car.

Lizzy thought for a moment and then began to understand. The web pattern she had worked on was the real Peg, and the body was just the car. The angel smiled and Lizzy became more confident about what she was about to do.

Together they stood at the foot of the bed and Lizzy closed her eyes, allowing herself to see through her hands. Inch by inch, she worked on repairing the splintered and shattered bones. As she needed tools, she would show an image in her mind to the angel and the angel would produce a tool from Lizzy's own experience. So, she worked with glue, scissors, bandages, staples, plaster, needle and thread. She meticulously gathered all the bits of shattered bone from Peg's hip and glued them back in place. Then she took her needle and thread and sewed the bones back in place.

She tied up tubes that were leaking; she reshaped disorganized organs and put them back in their correct position as the angel guided her. The ones that were really badly damaged were beyond her ability to fix and the angel handed her new ones still wrapped in plastic wrap with labels on. She looked at the packages in surprise and then carefully opened them before slipping the new organs in place. None of what she was doing seemed strange or fanciful to Lizzy as she worked hard with her sleeves rolled up.

Finally, she came to Peg's face, which had been badly disfigured by the impact. Inch by inch Lizzy remolded Peg's face, replacing the damaged eye and restructuring the cheekbones. The only thing she could not quite manage to get right was Peg's nose. No matter how hard she tried to mold, manipulate and reshape Peg's nose, it would not go back to its original shape. It worked again, like new, but it looked strange. Lizzy was beginning to get upset with herself when the angel intervened and told her to leave it alone.

"That would be Peg's reminder of this important time in her life. Just leave it. It is beyond your control. You can only work on parts of the body that want to be worked on, and the nose wants to stay that way."

The thoughts of the angel drifted around Lizzy's thoughts, and she removed her hands from Peg, feeling that the work was complete.

But the angel had not finished with Lizzy, even though Lizzy was exhausted. He propelled her back around to Peg's head and told her to put her hands delicately on Peg's skull. It took all her energy just to lift her hands and place them on her sister's head. Nothing happened. The angel told her to take all weight off of her hands so that she could feel more finely through her fingers. Lizzy did as she was asked.

Slowly, Lizzy became aware of a minute motion in the skull beneath her fingers. The angel showed Lizzy how the skull was divided into segments and how each segment should move freely from the others, as though floating in a tank of water. He showed her the movement forwards and backwards, and then side to side. She moved the plates of the skull around until she got used to the feel.

"Now," said the angel. "Feel where the plates have to go."

His words reverberated through her mind as she tuned herself into the head below her fingers. Gently, her fingers began to move, guiding the plates back to where they belonged, freeing up the pressure that had built up and trapped vital fluids. When everything was in place, she felt the angel pass into Peg and Lizzy went along with him.

He traveled up and down the length of Peg's body on what felt like a very gentle wave motion. She could feel instinctively that the wave was not strong enough to hold life and the angel dipped and moved, causing the wave to become stronger.

Together, they flowed in and out on a building tide that passed around Peg.

When the wave was at the appropriate strength, they withdrew from Peg, leaving Lizzy holding Peg's head. The angel detached from Lizzy and stood behind her. Before she could take her hands off her sister, a power pushed through her with horrific force before passing into her sister. The energy flowed through Lizzy into her sister, filling her with light and life.

The strength traveled around Peg's body, renewing her. As it passed through Lizzy it flowed into her also, feeding her body and replacing the energy that she had used up while helping her sister.

Finally, the energy flow stopped, and Lizzy fell to her knees. The angel picked her up and placed her back in her body that was still sleeping at the side of the bed. The angel then ran his hands over the child to harmonize her body so that she might adjust to the power and strain that she had carried.

The angel then began to turn. He turned with his arms outstretched to the heavens as he opened the Void within himself. He whispered many songs as he turned, and the songs stayed in the room as the angel vanished back into the Void.

Lizzy was in a deep sleep when her mother entered the hospital room after consulting with the doctor. It had taken her quite a while to compose herself before having to face her younger daughter. The doctor had said days rather than hours. That is all that would be left for her precious daughter. She had not screamed nor cried out when the doctor had told her this. She had expected him to tell her that Peg was going to die, and she was terrified that she would not be able to control herself.

But when the moment came, she had not felt anything. The words had not penetrated her mind until she left the room. Then she had shaken from head to toe. The ward sister had seen Mrs. Connor shaking in the corridor and she had herded her into the office. A hot cup of sweet tea had been placed in her hand, and she had been ordered to drink it. The sweetness mingled with the bitter pain in her heart, cutting through the silence and forcing her to cry. The crying had come gently, not the torrential force she had expected, but a simple release of built-up pressure.

How was she going to tell Lizzy? Peg was the center of Liz's universe. They fought like cat and dog, and Peg was constantly moaning about having to drag Lizzy everywhere with her. But Lizzy modeled her whole life around Peg and how Peg did things. Peg wore blue? Lizzy would dart back into her bedroom and change into something blue.

Her mother now stood on the threshold of the door and watched her sleeping daughter clinging onto Peg with her fingertips as Peg labored under the regime of the machines. She was about to go and wake Lizzy when something told her not to move or speak. Her deep instincts surfaced, telling her to stay where she was and not make a sound. So she leaned against the door threshold and observed her youngest daughter as she twitched in her dreams.

Peg lay as though already dead. Nothing moved unless the ventilator forced it, no sign of life offered itself from her broken body. It seemed like an age before Lizzy finally woke up and glanced around the room somewhat disoriented. Her mother smiled at her and slid quietly into the room, pulling up a chair to sit alongside her two most precious loves in the world.

"Mummy, Peg is going to be all right now, the angel told me. We fixed Peggy like new. Can she come home with us tomorrow?"

Lizzy's reedy voice sliced through Mrs. Connor's heart, leaving a raw wound to throb and bleed. Mrs. Connor bit her lip and pulled Lizzy onto her knee. Lizzy knew that something terrible was coming. Her mother only took her on her knee to tell her things that were going to hurt.

"Peg is very sick. She may not get better, so we have to pray for her. I want you to be a grown-up girl and be brave for me. Can you do that?"

Lizzy nodded and looked deeply into her mother's eyes.

"You don't believe me when I tell you that an angel has fixed Peggy and she will be home next week. You don't believe me, do you?"

Lizzy threw the accusation at her mother and slid off her knee, putting her hand to her mouth to chew her nails. She tried not to listen as her mother spoke to her.

"Lizzy, even if she were to get better, there is no way that she would be home next week. She will be here for months if she pulls through."

Lizzy looked in anger at her mother and then turned her back on her, facing the wall rather than look at the disbelief in her mother's eyes. Everyone treated her like a silly child, and it made her so mad. She wanted to be grown up and clever like Peg.

Her thoughts of Peg turned her to her sister who lay silently on the bed. She ran her hands over Peg's cheeks before her mother could stop her. She kissed her sister slowly and carefully before walking out of the room and sitting in the waiting room for her mother to take her home.

That night Lizzy burned with a fever. Her voice cried out through the darkness for her mother as her throat exploded in pain. Mrs. Connor turned the light on and stood for a second in shock as she

saw her daughter sitting up in bed crying. Her face was so red it looked burned. She held up her hands to her mother to show her the burns and blisters. Mrs. Connor fled to the phone and called the doctor.

Lizzy lay back in her bed, crying from the pain and exhaustion as her mother frantically shouted at the doctor to come as quickly as possible. Somewhere, something made Lizzy think of the angel and she silently called out to him to be with her.

She immediately felt his hands on her head, soothing his way through her as he slowed her tears.

"Do not be afraid, this will go soon enough. It is where the power has passed through you. One day, when you are older, you will learn to heal without such pain. But for now, be with it and allow it to fade in its own time. It will not harm you. Be blessed, little one who gave of herself."

The doctor arrived an hour or so later and Lizzy strained to hear the hushed tones in the hallway. She heard the words, *attention*, and *sympathy*, and wondered what they were talking about.

The doctor smiled as he sat at the side of her bed. He turned her hands slowly this way and that as he looked at the burns on her palms. He then brushed her hair from her face as he looked at her bright red cheeks. He asked her about fires and matches. Lizzy told him that she had been nowhere near anything like that because it was dangerous.

"So how do you manage to burn yourself, little Lizzy? I think your Mummy has enough to worry about without you getting ill too, don't you think?"

The doctor's voice was very calm. They did not believe her when she told them that the angel burned her; her mother just frowned and went out of the room. The doctor dressed the burns carefully and gave Lizzy a tablet for the pain. He told Lizzy's mum that he would arrange for the burns to be looked at tomorrow at the hospital.

Next morning, Mrs. Connor pushed through the crowd of three doctors and the staff nurses as she entered the ICU ward that housed Peg. They were crowded around Peg's bed and Mrs. Connor feared the worse. She pushed herself through to find Peg lying awake, talking in halting tones to the doctor. She turned upon hearing her mother's voice and began to cry. Mrs. Connor pushed a nurse out of the way and sat beside Peg, stroking her hair and trying not to cry. She looked up at the doctor in question and he raised his arms up with a smile on his face.

"I just don't understand it. One minute she was deep in a coma with little chance, and now? Now she looks good. Could I talk with you for a minute?"

The doctor steered Mrs. Connor into his office and Lizzy slid into the chair at the side of Peg's bed. Lizzy looked at her sister and Peg wearily looked back.

"I dreamed of you, you little snot."

Peg's voice was weak and scraping but the words brought a huge grin to Lizzy`s face.

"I dreamt you were fixing me up like you do with your Barbie dolls. I was covered in bandages and cream. God, I can't go anywhere or do anything without you being there."

Peg coughed and closed her eyes. Lizzy's smile widened to her whole body as she blossomed under the insulting compliments from her sister. It was her way of telling Lizzy that she was so happy to see her. This was their code of sisterhood.

Lizzy watched as the nurses fiddled with drips, needles and machines. She knew now that her sister would get better and that the angel did indeed heal her sister.

The doctor leaned back on his chair and fiddled with his pen. His eyebrows crunched together as he tried to find the words to explain what had happened to Peg.

"Your daughter is very strong and healthy and is recovering way beyond our expectations. We always try to lean on the downside when offering diagnosis, so that happenings like this, when we manage to pull someone through, are a nice surprise. She is still not out of danger and do not be fooled by her quick recovery. She is still a very ill child who has a lot of healing to do and lots of hurdles to jump. But it certainly looks better for Peg than it did last night."

Mrs. Connor was so happy for her daughter that she wanted to hug the doctor and spin him around, but she decided that he probably would not appreciate such a show of emotion, so she thanked him profusely for what he had done for her daughter.

"Oh, by the way doctor, my younger daughter, Lizzy, burned her hands yesterday and she has to have them redressed today. Which department do I take her to?"

Mrs. Connor had almost forgotten about Lizzy's burned hands. Her face had returned to a normal color this morning, which was a relief. The doctor gave her directions and asked what had happened to Lizzy. Mrs. Connor looked at her shoes.

"I think the stress of what happened got to Lizzy. She is a strange child and can be very difficult to handle sometimes. She lives in a dream world half the time. I think she burned them purposely so that she could be in hospital with Peg. Anyway, she seemed well enough this morning, and now that Peg is awake, it will help Lizzy to deal with all this. Thank you again, doctor."

Lizzy had to almost run to keep up with her mother as they marched down the maze of corridors that led to the outpatient department. When their turn finally came, Lizzy trotted forward to the nurse who started to unravel the dressing that the doctor had put on the night before. At the same time, the nurse was looking at the doctor's note, reading the details of his findings.

"Oh love. It sounds like you burned them good and proper. Do they still hurt? We will get them fixed up for you."

The nurse chatted to Lizzy as she clipped off the final layer of gauze that protected the deep burns that the doctor had found. The dressing was carefully lifted with tweezers and the nurse peeked underneath. She frowned and Mrs. Connor leaned forward in panic. The nurse lifted the hand up to the light. There was not a mark on the hand, only slight redness where the burns had been. The nurse turned the hand this way and that in confusion. Mrs. Connor looked to the nurse in question and Lizzy smiled.

"I told you Mummy; I told you the angel said it would be OK. Just like I told you that Peg was better and you didn't believe me."

Mrs. Connor apologized to the nurse for wasting her time and swept Lizzy off her feet and out of the examination room. Lizzy protested loudly until her mother pushed her through the bathroom door and plonked Lizzy down.

"OK, tell me all. What are you talking about and don't give me any more stories; I have run out of patience with all that."

Lizzy looked at her hands and then back at her mother. She could not remember much herself, but she told her mother, in low tones, about her dream as she slept alongside Peg. She told her about her body burning from the strain and the angel telling her that all would be well. She reminded her mother that she had known about the accident before anyone. She started to cry from frustration. No one ever believed her, just because she was ten.

Mrs. Connor bent down and hugged the child. Her common sense told her that what her daughter had told her was rubbish. But her instincts and the evidence told a different story. She knew when she was in the doctor's office that he had no clue what had helped Peg; he was as surprised as she was. Something within her did not want to acknowledge this child's claims but she knew that she had to.

"Lizzy, my love, I believe you. Now come on, we have to go and see Peg before she loses that terrible temper of hers."

Mrs. Connor spoke the words deliberately and slowly, hoping to God that she was not doing something she would regret later.

CHAPTER 4
THE BOOK OF DEATH

PART ONE

Margaret brushed the stray hair from her face and looked out over the washing line. Her tired arms drooped onto the thick line and rested there for a second. Hanging washing always hurt her arms and today it was worse than ever. With a groan, she bent over and tried to pick up a peg that she had dropped on the damp grass. Her toes gripped the earth as she tried to balance, but to no effect. She tipped forward from the weight of her body and landed on her knees.

"You should squat; it's much better for you than bending."

The interfering voice cut through Margaret's wet maternity shirts that hung haphazardly on the line and moved slowly with the light breeze. The voice jumped over the fence and parted the damp washing.

"Here, come on, up you get."

The young man from next-door put his hands under Margaret's arms and heaved her onto her feet in one swift movement. It was too fast for Margaret, causing her to become dizzy. She clung onto him, trying to stop herself from swaying.

How dare he tell her what to do and then stick his hands in her armpits? Her face reddened with embarrassment and the cursed panic crept upon her. She felt sick. She did not want to throw up in front of this idiot, so she clung to him, gulping for air.

"S'cuse me for asking, but how far on are you? You look pretty big; are you carrying twins?" The young man's voice cut through Margaret like a knife through butter.

That finally cured Margaret of her nausea. She wanted to launch into him for being so rude, but she knew she would not be able to pluck up the courage. Deep within her she knew that he was

just trying to be friendly, and he had helped her. What had gotten into her just lately? Everything annoyed her, everything frightened her; everything made her want to scream.

Her chin jutted out as she looked up at the bright teen face that smiled back at her. "I'm thirty-five weeks, five more weeks to go. No, it's not twins, I'm just big."

The young man became uncomfortable. He slowly realized that he had probably insulted her by saying that she was big. It was beginning to dawn on him that women did not like things like size pointed out to them. He had often wanted to talk to her, not for any, well, sexual reason, but because she always seemed so alone.

Her husband only seemed to come home one or two days a week and even then, he would arrive, park up his large truck and then go out in his car. He never seemed to take her anywhere and she never seemed to go out very much.

As he looked closer at her face, it became clear to him that she was not that much older than him, probably only a year or two. She looked around twenty and his eighteenth birthday was only a month away.

"Well, I'll leave you to it then. Please, call over the fence if you need anything."

The young man smiled awkwardly before bounding back over the fence. Margaret placed her hands under her armpits where he had gripped to lift her. Now that she had recovered from the indignity of being a beached whale flapping about on the ground, she savored the moment of human contact.

That night, as in all nights just recently, her dreams came harsh and unrelenting. She tossed around in her bed, entangling herself in the soft blue cotton sheets, and her black hair mingled with the blue in the still silent darkness. Her arms twitched as she recoiled away from something: the dark fear slowly tiptoed towards her, taunting her.

Beads of sweat and panic broke out on her forehead as she inched away from the unseen, her closed eyes darting this way and that in an effort to find safety. The sound of her breathing punctured the silence as it became more urgent, her breath laboring against the inner terror.

She lay rigid and motionless for a few seconds before her hands flew to her face, her fingers trying to fight something off. Margaret's voice called out into the darkness and her eyes opened suddenly. Her body was paralyzed. Her hands were still by her face, unable to move.

The darkness took shape and moved towards her. Her body prickled against the fear as the being moved ever so slowly to her side. She could not turn her head, nor could she cry out.

It approached her, growing until it extended beyond the ceiling. Each hair on her body told her to run. The droplets of sweat that ran down her face and breasts told her to scream. But her body lay motionless against the horror that moved slowly in a deliberate path towards her.

She struggled to move her eyes from side to side. The being had filled the whole room and she knew in her heart it was something that she could not escape. Its hand reached out to touch her.

It was aiming for her forehead. She knew she had to stop it but she did not know how. The child in her womb lay motionless, as though waiting for the inevitable. Her instincts were to put her arms around her swollen belly and protect the little child snuggled up within her, but her arms remained glued around her head.

Just before it reached her forehead, she knew, from somewhere deep within her, that if it touched her, she would die. She did not want to die. She wanted her baby. She began to cry helplessly, for herself and her unborn child. The tears touched her face and something snapped within her.

Her eyes opened and an inrush of air to her lungs made her jump. Sleep fell away from her as she sat up in bed, covered in sweat and tears. Her arms embraced her face as she wept, unable to cope with yet another night of the same nightmare.

PART TWO

"Okay, that's it, Mrs. Kingsley, is there anything you want to ask?"

The doctor stood smiling at Margaret, but she could see from the look on his face that he really did not want her to ask anything. But she knew she had to say something. Margaret smiled at the nurse who had done her weekly observations, checking Margaret's blood pressure, urine and a mountain of other seemingly useless things.

"Well, there is one thing."

Her voice was unsteady as she began to redden. She felt overpowered by this professional man who held life and death and her health in his hands.

The doctor looked briefly at the ceiling and then back at Margaret before smiling. He had spent three minutes with this woman and now it was time for her to go. He hated women who asked questions. Why could they not just come in, be examined and get lost? His words came out with thinly disguised impatience, making Margaret go even redder.

"Go ahead, ask."

Margaret fiddled with her thumbs and tried to sound as confident as possible.

"Well, I feel that there is something wrong. The feeling gets stronger every day, but I don't know what it is. I just don't feel right."

She dropped her head and looked at her hands. She felt like such an idiot for blurting that out. The doctor looked at the rotund, red-faced, raven-haired young woman sitting in a lump before him. He could see that she must have been quite pretty before she got pregnant, but they all faded after the babies started. It was always the same. That, he thought to himself, is why he would never marry.

"Mrs. Kinglsey, there is nothing wrong with you. Your blood pressure is a little high, but that's okay. Now stop worrying, it will do baby no good at all if you worry. All will be well."

The nurse stood by the door with it open and smiled at Margaret. "Good-bye, Mrs. Kingsley."

The nurse continued to smile until the smile became fixed. Margaret slid from the chair and heaved herself up. Her body felt more than heavy, it felt poisoned. Her whole being seemed to be under a cloud and no one wanted to help or listen. As the nurse closed the door behind her, Margaret heard her voice filter through to the hallway.

"God, some of these women are such hypochondriacs."

Margaret wanted to cry. She felt violated and humiliated, and she could not find within her the strength to challenge these people. Her mother had always told her that when twenty-one arrived, she would find her voice. But it had not happened. Here she was, twenty-one, and she dare not say boo to anyone.

She cursed herself all the way home as she trudged back up the steep hill that led to her house. The road was dirty and smelly, full of rubbish that people had thrown from their cars. That was how she felt: just a piece of rubbish that someone had thrown from a car.

She leaned heavily on the door when she finally arrived home. She had to wait a moment to summon the strength to get the key in the lock, and when she finally got herself in, she knew she would have to go to bed for the afternoon to recover from the walk and the insults. Her nights were full of terror, and she awoke every morning full of fear and exhaustion. At least she did not dream when she slept during the day.

She lay back on the bed, fully clothed, staring at the ceiling. She placed her hand on her enormous belly and caressed the child within her. Tigger, her secret name for her baby, had not moved in days. The doctor said it was normal. She felt that something was wrong.

Tigger was named Tigger because of Tigger's amazing ability to do back flips at the most inconvenient moment. Tigger kicked, squirmed, hiccupped, pushed, stretched and generally gave a little joy and humor to Margaret in her loneliness. But now Tigger had stopped communicating with her. She felt the child was still alive, there were tiny little wriggles here and there, but nothing like what she had grown used to.

Slowly, Margaret drifted into sleep, her body twitching as she descended down into the underworld, leaving her conscious mind behind. The dark stillness swallowed her until her jaw finally relaxed. The sleep was delicious. It drank its way through her body and the softness of the bed became deeper, kinder and full of warmth; something that she had not felt in a long time.

When her eyes finally began to open, just as the sun was

going down, her body snuggled into the comfort, lying and enjoying as she slowly surfaced from a rest that had not been plagued with terror and pain. In fact, for the first time in a long time, she felt no pain at all. She moved her legs to stretch and became aware that the bed was damp. She moved her leg back, and yes, there was dampness.

She stretched her arm out to turn on the lamp and she sat up in bed. As she sat up, pain from hell shot through her, causing her to scream suddenly and fall backwards back onto the bed. She lay panting for a moment. Surely it was too early for her waters to break and the labor to start? She eased herself back up, slowly this time, allowing the pain to build rather than to attack. She pulled the bedcovers back, and cried out. The bed was soaked in blood.

Her hand reached calmly for the bedside phone and dialed the emergency number. She talked so calmly that she could hear the disbelief in the dispatcher's voice. She replaced the receiver after being assured that an ambulance was on its way.

Lying back on the bed, she felt no panic, no fear. Everything was OK. Everything would be fine. There was no problem; it was all under control. She slowly sat back up and tried to stand. She felt dizzy but not too bad.

Methodically she peeled off her bloodstained clothes and looked for fresh ones. The bleeding had stopped and she began to feel silly for calling an ambulance. Maybe she really did not need one. By the time the ambulance arrived, she had dressed herself, packed a small hospital case and left a note for her husband. She had also left a message on his work answering machine, just in case someone could manage to get a message to him.

The ambulance man helped her into the vehicle and an ambulance woman wrapped a blanket around her. There was no sign of blood, no stains, no new fresh blood: just a tired heavily pregnant woman who was slightly embarrassed at the fuss. They set off, and as they traveled the woman took some details. She looked Margaret up and down, looking for signs of bleeding, shock, anything. Nothing.

"Are you alone? I mean, when will your husband get back from work? Is there anyone we can call?"

Margaret shook her head. The woman nodded and eyed Margaret again: another lonely one looking for attention. She wrote that down as a side note on the admittance paper and circled it.

At the maternity unit, Margaret eased herself onto the bed and retold what had happened as the nurses listened quietly. They nodded without comment and then asked Margaret to undress and put on a hospital gown. One of the nurses picked up Margaret's underwear and stated to the head nurse that there was no sign of bleeding.

"But there was a lot of blood in the bed, honestly there was."

Margaret was beginning to despair. It seemed that no one believed her. She looked from face to face as they all smiled patronizingly at her.

"Well, Mrs. Kingsley, we will link you up to a monitor to see what's happening and we will listen to the baby. You say he hasn't been moving? Well, that's natural at the end of a pregnancy; don't worry about it. We will also do some tests to see what's happening. Just lay back and relax, doctor will be with you shortly."

Margaret lay on the hospital bed staring out at the other women who all lay staring at her and the wall. The place was depressing with no one talking and no one smiling. She lay there for over an hour and was just dozing into the night softness when a brusque nudge of the bed brought her back to the gloomy ward.

She groaned inwardly when she recognized the clinic doctor who stood before her. She could also see from his face that he was groaning inwardly too. Another hypochondriac had dragged him away from golf practice in the locker room.

He sat on the side of the bed and looked her over. He asked about the monitor and the nurse informed him that there was not a low priority one available until the morning. He nodded and asked Margaret to `scoot` down the bed. She looked at him blankly.

"Please lie down and I will check your cervix to see if it is dilating–to see if you are in labor."

She lay down and the doctor pulled the bedclothes back. She did not register his face change at first, nor did she think it strange that the nurse had scurried off. She felt warm, relaxed and comfortable. Another nurse appeared with a large pad, which she slipped under Margaret's bottom. Margaret looked at her questioningly.

"For the blood." The nurse's voice was curt and to the point.

The nurse did not elaborate and Margaret peered between her legs. Blood oozed out of her, slowly building into a pool between her legs. Strange, thought Margaret, I didn't feel it this time. In fact, as she plopped her hand on her leg to lever herself up, she had not felt that either. She wiggled her toes and breathed a sigh of relief that she could move them, except she could not feel her left leg or foot. Monitors appeared from nowhere and wires were soon growing out of every nook and cranny of her body.

"I'm going to break your waters and we are putting up a drip to help speed up your labor. We would normally do a section on you, an operation, but we have no spare theater for nearly four hours at least. There is no emergency and all is well; the drip will really speed things up and he will be out in no time," said the doctor.

He tried to sound as confident as possible. He hated the

national health, he hated working in this hellhole and as soon
as he was able, he wanted to leave England forever, maybe to
work in one of the Arab states where all the money was.
Margaret caught hold of his wrist and looked into his eyes.

"Is my baby OK? It's a little early, isn't it?"

Margaret wanted to panic, but she could not. She felt calm
and safe, but she knew she had to ask. The doctor looked at her
wearily. He tried to sound as strong as he could as he answered
her searching question.

"No, lots of babies are born at this time, all will be well.
Now you relax, you have a busy night ahead of you."

She lay back on her pillow and smiled at the nurse who had
been stationed to watch over her. There was also someone
standing behind her. But Margaret was not able to make out
the figure that stood silent and unmoving.

She drifted off, unaware of the painless tightening that was
stirring in her belly. The bleeding had stopped yet again,
allowing everyone to breathe a sigh of relief. The warmth
spread around her and pulled her deeper and deeper into a
semi-sleep, the regular beeping of the machines singing her
into oblivion.

The pain rose like a submarine surfacing from deep water,
catching her unawares and making her gasp. The monitor
sounds became uneven and somewhere, someone was
shouting.

Margaret opened her eyes and looked through the haze of
pain. The doctor's face peered back at her, along with the
nurses and her midwife, who had just arrived and looked a
little flustered. Behind the nurse and midwife stood two other
people, but the shadows seemed to hide their features.

It never occurred to Margaret that the ward was in full light
and that there were no shadows. More and more people
pushed around her, whispering to her, coaxing her.

Margaret, Margaret, come see the flowers, come see the lilies, they are so beautiful.

Margaret wanted to tell the voice that she was too busy having a baby to look at flowers, but her lips did not seem to work. The pain rose again, filling the space that she breathed and clearing out of her mind any thought other than pain: endless ceaseless pain. It got stronger and stronger as she groaned, the noise coming from deep within her. Someone touched her belly and Margaret wanted to pull the hands away, but her arms were too heavy to pick up.

Sounds rushed past her, hands touched her, and faces peered through the fog in her mind, staring at her intently. Someone told her to roll onto her side, but she did not know what that meant. What is a side?

She felt her body being pushed over onto her left side. The pain grew tentacles and seemed to grab her around her throat. Her breath became shorter until all she could do was grunt. Her thoughts became her world as she bathed in memories punctured only by pain as it passed through on its way to somewhere.

A pressure began to build up in her head. At the same time, something solid moved down from her belly into her pelvis. The fullness became a center point for the pain, which was now exquisite as she bathed in it. Someone shouted her name. Again and again. "Margaret, Margaret!"

She stood and looked at the chaos that was happening in the room. She found it much easier to breath now that she was no longer laid on the bed. Someone else was laid there. Margaret edged closer and froze when she recognized the woman on the bed. She looked at herself laying there, with her legs flayed and her lower body covered in blood.

One of the nurses was crying as she carried something wrapped in a green cloth that the doctor had handed to her. Margaret peered to see what it was. The body of a stillborn infant lay in the nurse's arms as she prepared a container. Margaret was confused.

She did not know why she could see herself on the bed when she was standing up and she did not know why they had a dead child. She hoped her child would not be born like that. She shuddered and thought about her own child. Should not she be busy with her labor?

With that thought she found herself back on the table and felt a warm wet cloth being wiped over her face. She heard beeping and alarms. She heard conversations and regrets. Margaret wanted to comfort the nurse who had been crying. She wanted to say, "Don't be sad, my baby will be born soon, and you will see how beautiful she is. She will make you smile."

But she was too cold to speak. It had crept quietly upon her and wound its way into her bones, lodging itself there. The warmth from the cloth that was washing her down did not seem to penetrate her cold and she wanted to ask a nurse for a blanket. But her lips would not work. She tried to lift her arm to catch their attention, but she could not move. So, she lay there while she was washed and thought about her child to come.

The daydream was shattered by a voice that cut through her cold and her thoughts. The doctor was speaking into a tape machine. He mentioned her name. He mentioned hemorrhage and torn placenta. He described the condition of the dead child. He listed a date and time of Margaret's death. February 14th, 3.45 a.m. Margaret screamed.

The cry rolled through her body yet it could not escape. So it turned inward, digging deep into her soul and tearing her into shreds. It dug and dug until there was nowhere else to go. And then came the blackness.

PART THREE

Margaret moved in the darkness. Her thoughts reached out through the nothing and yet that nothing was full of everything. Someone called her. They did not use her name, or so she thought. But it was a sound that identified her, and in her fear and loneliness, she moved towards that sound.

The sound got louder until she found herself before a door. There seemed to be no door, but she knew it was there. She also knew that she had to go through that door. And yet, she was not sure as to who or what she was. What part of her was going to go through that door?

The urge to move forward grew stronger and stronger until, using thought, she passed through the doorway and felt the power of transition as she crossed the threshold. It was like waking from one of her terrible dreams. Her eyes scanned the horizon of a seemingly never-ending desert shining in the noonday sun.

In the far distance was a range of mountains and Margaret set off walking. The sun tore into her flesh as she walked, her feet stumbling as her legs got heavier and heavier. At first, it did not seem strange to her that she should be in a desert. But the further she walked, the more the memory of the hospital bed came back.

She remembered the pain and her child. She remembered her ever-absent husband and she remembered, finally, the voice of the doctor dictating his notes into a tape recorder. Margaret Kingsley, date and time of death: February 14th, 3.45 a.m. What a shame, he had said, to die birthing your first child on Valentine's Day.

The knowledge of her death washed over her, and she began to weep. Her feet dragged over the dry earth and her tears fell, joining with other tears to form a stream that trickled on into the distance.

Without noticing, she had come closer to the mountains, and Margaret looked up into the distance. The stream of tears ran ahead of her and joined into a river that sliced through the landscape. Up to now, she had felt no thirst. But on seeing the river, her throat began to burn with the fire of the desert, consuming all her thoughts.

As she came close to the river, she realized that she was not alone in the desert. People wandered about on the river's edge, some staring into space. Others lay weeping, their hands covering their faces. The sorrow of the people blew past her like the wind, catching her off guard. The emotions flowed through her, contracting her heart in pain.

The loss of her own child began to swell within her and instinctively she placed her hand on her abdomen. Her husband's neglect of her rose to greet her, along with the scorn that her father had always directed at her.

Memories of her childhood surfaced, memories of pain and of joy. Things that she did not want to let go of. Her cats and her house paraded before her and Margaret began to feel homesick. She wanted to go home.

Immediately she found herself standing in her lounge. But it was full of people. Her husband sat in his usual armchair with his head cradled in his hands. Beside him sat his mother with her arm, as always, protecting her son. Margaret felt instant overwhelming jealousy.

His mother always had to interfere, always had to side with him to protect him, even when he had done wrong. Mummy would always make it better. The bitterness simmered in Margaret as she stared at the plump, overdressed woman.

Another man walked into the room, her husband's brother. He had hated Margaret on sight. The feeling had been mutual. He walked up to her husband and squatted on the floor beside him.

"We all will miss her; we all loved her."

His voice quivered as his younger brother looked up in thanks for the kind words. Margaret wanted to be sick. Not only did she know he was lying, but she could see the lies floating out of him. She saw the smugness nestled next to his heart and she wanted to tear it out for all to see.

Someone sniffled behind her, prompting Margaret to turn around. There, in black, with deep rings under her eyes sat Tanya, her best friend. Tanya had been working abroad and had flown back for the funeral. Margaret felt the horrendous pain that Tanya carried within her. She could hear Tanya's thoughts as she mulled over the fact that Margaret would probably be alive today if she had not moved away, but had stayed close to be with her friend during her pregnancy.

Tanya had, right at the beginning of the pregnancy, a premonition that something was going to happen, and she had ignored it. The guilt tore into Tanya and Margaret wanted to ease that.

She moved next to her friend and placed her arms around her. She whispered into her ear while stroking her hair. How would she ever let go of her deepest love, her friend from childhood? All that remained of her memories of childhood happiness was Tanya. She would stay with her forever.

At first, she did not notice the man who stood silently in the corner of the room. He was dressed strangely with a black hat and a long beard. Margaret wondered if he was a vicar. She did not recognize him. Then he looked at her. Margaret was startled. How could he see her? He stared and stared at Margaret until she spoke to him.

"Who are you? How can you see me?"

The man did not answer but walked towards her. When he got to the table, he walked through the table and straight to Margaret. She tried to run.

"You have no legs, how can you run? And where to? Come, follow me, I want to show you something."

He held out his hand and she grasped it without question. They were back at the side of the river and Margaret became angry with the man.

"Why have you brought me back here? I don't want to be here; I want to be with my friend." She struggled against him but he held her firmly with his eyes.

"You do not belong there, that is not your world and that is not your friend. It has all gone and will never return. You must let go and cease to be Margaret Kingsley. You must be yourself."

Margaret cried out through her fear.

"I *am* Margaret, what are you talking about?"

She wanted to flee but she could not move, and she did not know where to flee. Instead, she flopped down to the ground, putting her head in her hands. All around her, people sat with their heads in their hands. Fear swam around them, lapping at their feet and refusing to go away.

Whenever she was in pain, Margaret always remembered her mother and the pain would go away. Her mother had died when she was a little girl, but Margaret had clung to the threads of memory that had remained with her.

Instantly she found herself back in her old childhood bedroom with her mother perched on the end of the bed, her golden hair shining from the hall light that reflected around her. Her mother smiled and Margaret snuggled down into bed. At last, she was safe and warm; no one could harm her.

But something was wrong. Her mother did not change her expression and did not read her a story like mothers are supposed to. She just sat and smiled the same smile that Margaret had always remembered: the only memory that she had of her mother. The memory played itself over and over until Margaret finally understood that she could not hide in her memories.

She was back again, by the river, with her head in her hands. She looked up and scanned the desert. People were constantly arriving out of the wilderness and sitting down by the river. Most ran to the river to drink, throwing the water over themselves and laying down to drink their fill. But Margaret did not want to do that. Yes, she had been thirsty, but something within her drove the thirst away.

People panicked around her; some cried out and others became violent. But the man who had frightened her with his words sat without emotion, looking out over the river with an expression of peace on his face. Margaret was intrigued. She walked over to him and sat quietly down beside him.

He did not react at first, but just allowed Margaret to be still with him as he watched the mountains. Finally, he turned to look at her. Margaret wanted to introduce herself properly, but for the moment, she could not remember her name.

"That is good," said the man.

"What is good?" said Margaret.

"That you do not hold to your name. It is time it was no longer with you. It was just a tool and now you have finished your job, you no longer need the tools."

The man's voice was beautiful, but she wasn't sure she understood what he said. She tried to change the subject.

"Who are you, and how come you are not so afraid?"

Margaret was curious; this man was like no other she had seen anywhere. And yet, he just looked like a rather crumpled old man.

"Oh, I am myself. I remember this place, it holds no fear for me, and you will remember next time around, because you were wise enough not to drink of the river."

Margaret opened her mouth to ask about his answer, and then shut it again. Maybe she should not ask.

"So, what did you do, you know, before, well, before you died?"

She tried to be polite, but the question came out sounding rude and she wanted to be angry at herself, except she could not remember how to. The old man smiled and pulled on his beard as he looked out over the mountains.

"Hmm, well, I was supposed to be recognized. But no one recognized me, so here we all are and here we go again."

Margaret frowned in confusion. She had no clue what he was talking about, and yet, something deep dawned within her. Rather than ignore it like she would normally do, she allowed it to rise in to her thoughts.

She saw the man in a beautiful city, like the pictures she had seen of Jerusalem. He was walking the streets and he shone like the August sun. But no one seemed to notice. Everything he touched became beautiful, every word he spoke took shape and traveled around him, echoing sounds out to the world. But no one heard. No one recognized the grace that poured from this man. Therefore no one could partake of that grace.

"I see," said Margaret.

Margaret felt sadness for the man, that no one had recognized him. But then, she felt that he had no sadness, so why should she? What purpose would it serve? Why would it have a place here?

"You learn quickly!" said the man as he smiled at her.

Margaret scanned the horizon silently. She was confused about many things, and the more she talked, the more confused she became. She turned back to the man, a question itching to be asked.

"OK, one last question. Where is God? And Jesus? I don't see any of the stuff we were taught about at school. Where are they? Do they exist?"

The man laughed loudly and then turned Margaret around. She did not know what she was looking at for a second. She watched a man walking towards the river and he was weeping uncontrollably. She could see pain all around him. Loss and regret fell as tears into his hands as he walked.

He reached out in all directions for something, anything to

guide him. A being, like a thread of light appeared and began walking towards the man. As the being got closer, it began to take human form. It formed itself into the image of Jesus and held out its arms for the man. The man saw Jesus and ran weeping towards him. The being enveloped him and held him in compassion until the man was ready to be released.

Margaret blanched. She had not led a religious life, not really. But she had been raised a Catholic and here she seemed to be seeing that Jesus was just a masquerading being. Her new friend heard the thought and shook his head.

"No, Jesus was a person who lived in time and then did not live in time. He was who he was, but he was not a crutch, as people would like to wish that he was. The eternal child of light who manifests in many different forms, one form as Jesus, is a timeless expression of divinity. But when people die, they often die in fear and they cling to whatever memory they have of something greater than themselves. So, the beings that are responsible for the transition of life and death, the doorways, often have to appear in a form taken from the human mind. These doorways, you know them as angels. Not long blond-haired men with wings, but beings who are a matrix for divine power. Doorways, thresholds, enablers."

His words made sense to Margaret, and yet thought was becoming difficult for her. She did not want to learn, or think. She wanted to do something, to move forward. She had started to feel uncomfortable, as though she did not fit anymore. Her body shape had started to break up and she was finding it harder to think of herself as a human shape.

She turned to ask the man about this feeling but as she formed the question, she already knew the answer. Her earthly body had been cremated. She had no material pattern left that she could connect to in solid form.

In the distance, a bridge appeared over the river. It was a bridge of light, shape, and movement that drew Margaret instinctively towards it. She wanted to ask about the bridge, but the man had vanished. She turned, looking all around her, but he was nowhere to be seen.

The bridge pulled harder and harder until she could not bear it any longer. She broke into a run, pulled by a deep urge that coursed its way through her, driving every other thought out of her mind. On reaching the threshold of the bridge she stopped suddenly. Something blocked her. She leaned against it, trying to break through.

The sound of a whirlwind whipped around her pushing at her from all directions, and she became frightened. Out of the whirlwind peered many eyes, focused intently on her and probing deep into her thoughts.

Memories flooded into her mind. Memories of her childhood, her early love affairs, her night terrors, her baby, and her death. But somehow, these memories did not evoke anything within her anymore. They seemed like lead weights that pulled her farther and farther away from the bridge. She did not want them, she no longer needed them, and so she let the whirlwind take them.

It tore into her, dismantling her of everything that she knew. It tore at her thoughts, her ideas, and the concepts she had learned with the man on the riverbank. It pulled away all her emotions and beliefs until she stood naked before its eyes.

The whirlwind stopped. All was quiet. It felt so wonderful to be rid of all the baggage she carried for so long, and with that lightness, she stepped forward onto the bridge.

The moment her foot touched the surface of the bridge something passed through her. For each step she took, she felt a joining with something, a communing, as though she had become part of a huge web that spread into infinity.

It felt good; it felt natural, as though this was her real self. The crest of the bridge drew her onwards, and passing over the center of the bridge, nothingness enfolded her. The nothingness had all the potential of everything in it. Every thought, deed, word, and universe was held like a breath in that nothingness.

She knew she had a choice. Stay in the nothingness, or move on in service. The nothingness beckoned to her. She could drink of the union with all Divine potential, being at one with the Void: the source of all creation. But something else pulled her in the opposite direction. Service. To be in a world, in a life, and allow life to flow through her. The act of being within substance. She chose substance.

Immediately she was back on the bridge, stepping through the connections of all worlds as she journeyed towards the threshold of the other side. With each step that she took, her awareness expanded to enfold each soul who had walked the path she was now walking. She felt the deep connection with each individual as they passed through and over the bridge in their own time and space. Like the web, they were all one being.

On reaching the other side, an angel pointed into the distance. Rising out of the earth was a huge range of mountains. The angel indicated that she must climb the biggest mountain.

Her heart sank. It was so far away and so high, she would never get all the way up there. The angel started to walk with her, placing one foot in front of the other, and she copied; one step at a time.

At the foot of the mountain, the angel vanished without any warning or communication, leaving Margaret to stare up at the clouds which covered the summit. A pathway was worn by footfalls as it snaked up the side of the mountain, vanishing into the mist.

Margaret stepped on the path and began to climb. She heard whispers and mumblings as she climbed. There was nothing specific that she could grasp, just noise. But the higher she climbed, the clearer the voices became.

She heard the texts of the gospels being read and the words mingled in with recitations of the Qu`ran. Over the top of that was a speaking of the Torah, the Gita, and beyond that a whispering of Fire incantations. Words in languages she had never heard muttered in the background. All the sacred words that had ever been written and uttered whispered around her, making it harder and harder to reach the top of the mountain.

Other voices joined in the chorus, voices raised in political anger, voices speaking out against beliefs, voices calling for war, cries for peace. And the loudest: the cry of beings as they were slaughtered to satisfy the hunger of other beings.

The cry broke through all others and imprinted itself on her. It followed her wherever she turned. She could not escape it. The cry echoed around the mountains, pleading with those who journeyed not to replay such an imbalance.

Margaret climbed and climbed in an attempt to escape the noise. As she neared the top, the sounds suddenly stopped. All was quiet; all was peaceful. The mist hid the summit from her and the atmosphere around her had become cold and damp. She knew she had to walk into the mist. She knew she could not turn around and return back down the mountain. There was nowhere else for her to go but into the unseen.

Her thoughts stilled as she prepared for what was beyond the mountain mist. The weight of her previous life had all but fallen away. It had become some dark distant memory that she had managed to finally shrug off like a disease. Now she was herself. Timeless.

With that stillness, she moved into the mist and was immediately enveloped in a dreadful weariness. Her mind forcibly pushed her onwards until she could go no further. The mist had begun to thin ever so slightly; just enough to see back down some of the mountain and to see ahead. Before her lay many people, all fast asleep. Beyond them, the mountaintop fell away but the mist obscured the horizon.

The tiredness ate into her and she fell to her knees. Motionless, she stayed in that position briefly, before finally laying down. Each position that she took felt uncomfortable until a voice passed through her.

"Remember," the voice said.

Remember what?

Margaret could not remember, but the body that she no longer had remembered. Its human imprint, which was stored deep within her, remembered. The memory played out through her and she shifted into the remembered position. On her stomach, left arm outstretched, right arm behind her back. Right leg outstretched, left leg bent and tucked behind right leg. Finally, she knew she was in the correct position. With that knowledge came sleep.

The keepers of the dead wandered in and out of the sleeping bodies, maintaining the sleeper's inner balance as they slept. Some that they came across still had residual patterns from their last life that needed removing. With their long hair-like fingers, the keepers combed through the bodies of those who slept, reorganizing and harmonizing that which was out of balance.

The keepers took pity on the sufferings of the sleepers. Some of the sleepers had passed through death in terror and had been driven back into rebirth by deep instinctive urges that they could not comprehend. But some of the souls had actually opted to stay in substance form, to serve humanity.

In their pity, the keepers lay beside those who slept and sang songs to them about the power of the Abyss. They sang songs that would settle in the minds of the sleepers and guide them during the darkest hours of their incarnations.

They stroked the sleepers, filling them with balance and power, tools they would need for their journey ahead. And finally, before the dawn of the sleepers broke, the keepers held the deep eternal inner flame of each sleeper and gave it sanctuary. The flame of divine being, waiting for its next expression in life.

As the dawn broke, the mist cleared. The keepers called to the dawn with a conch shell—the labyrinth of the ocean that carries the wind. The noise awoke the sleepers who looked out in awe as the light and darkness of the Void shone upon them.

Margaret turned in the blackness, at one with the nothing. Not wishing to move or be. Silence. Out of the silence, the sound of a loud horn vibrated through her, calling her back to existence. Margaret wanted to fight the call, she wanted to stay within the stillness, but the call became more and more urgent.

She awoke to find herself lying on the top of a mountain. She looked up just in time to see someone bend over and push her down the far side of the mountain. She wanted to cry out in panic, but her breath was taken as she rolled and tumbled down what felt like a grassy hill.

During the rolling, she became more and more aware that she was feeling with senses and shape; with limbs, eyes, ears, even though she had none. The strangeness of such thoughts tumbled with her as she cascaded down the hill. The scent of the fresh grass and dust awoke her awareness of the world and of being in human form. She ached for such life again and just as the ache became unbearable, something slowed her to a stop.

She unraveled herself at the foot of the hill and stood up. Before her was a large rupture in the ground—the Abyss. Behind her was the mountain. Looking up, she could see others tumbling down, just as she had done.

They all slowed, seemingly of their own accord, until something nudged them from behind. The nudge seemed to alter Margaret's vision, and she slowly became aware of a giant hand reaching out to each person and carefully slowing him or her down. She turned back to look at the Abyss and before it stood a being that made Margaret very afraid.

Before the Void stood an angelic being that reached up to the stars. She had many arms and wings that stretched out to prevent people from falling into the Abyss. Many other arms reached out to slow those who tumbled down the hill. Her hair flowed in all directions, scooping up those who had lost their way. Her eyes turned to each person as she looked at them intently, one by one.

Her eyes finally looked into Margaret and Margaret began to cry. Every failing that she had, became apparent to her. Every cruelty, ignorance, indifference, stupidity and thoughtlessness paraded before her. Behind it came every goodness, every drop of love that she had shed for others, every hand she had outstretched, every gift she had given.

The angel weighed it all in the palm of her hand. The balance was presented without judgment back to Margaret and Margaret became aware of what she needed to achieve to better that balance.

The angel turned her head to look out over the Abyss and Margaret's gaze followed. She saw many lives paraded in front of her, all lives that would give her the skills to achieve what she needed. Some were more tempting than others, but Margaret could see that the tempting ones might not yield all that she needed in a balanced way.

She saw one life that she felt she recognized. It was a difficult life and yet was rich in learning. Her heart lurched towards it and Margaret followed. The angel withdrew the protective arm from Margaret's center and Margaret pitched forward into the Abyss.

A whirlwind came up to greet her and whipped her into its center. Her thoughts were flung around and around the directions as she fell, its wind flowing through her and adjusting her for what was to come.

The angel stood impassive as the couple joined in love. The emotions that they released for each other joined and created a vortex, spinning throughout the worlds. The vortex connected with a whirlwind that whipped out of the Abyss, and the roar of the whirlwind echoed around the room where the couple lay. Still the angel did not move.

At the moment of connection between the vortex and the whirlwind, a light shone through the darkness and the angel began to awaken from its stillness. A soul tumbled through the worlds, twisting and turning within the whirlwind as the soul passed from wind to vortex. The whirlwind withdrew and the soul completed its birthing into the world as it slowly passed, guided by the angel, into the body of the woman lying in the arms of her lover.

On contact, the soul spread out, joining with the soul of the woman and the angel took its position by her head. A beautiful web pattern appeared, the pattern of human shape. The angel gently teased the newly arrived soul into the pattern and wove it in deftly within the pattern of the mother.

The woman's body shone with the intricate connections as her soul upheld and gave sanctuary to the new being that would eventually be her child. When the angel was satisfied that the connection was complete, it withdrew and vanished into the Void.

Margaret turned in a swirl of warmth and love. A regular heartbeat punched out a sense of rhythm for her as she lay in light. She was at one with being in substance and yet she was in the stillness, in the deep. It was a place she did not want to leave, ever.

But there came a time, a turning within her. The sense of connection was lessening, and her sense of being was growing. She became aware that she was not her surroundings; that they were separate from her, and yet were still a part of her. At that point, the moment of awareness of separate, something shifted with her. She knew she had to leave. But to where?

The urge for a journey became overwhelming. It tore at her, forcing her to make the move to leave. Once the thought was accepted, her world began to contract and change. Pressure built up all around her, forcing her, squashing her into a battle for life.

She tried to fight back at times, until a deep knowing within her surfaced, telling her to relax. She felt herself leave the safety and comfort of her world. There was only forward into the unknown, there was nowhere else to go. It was terrifying. Her mind reached forward as her body was propelled on until she broke free of the warmth and safety into a dull brightness full of external noise and coldness. She took a breath as her thoughts vanished into the brightness and the loneliness of separation hit her without mercy.

The angel hovered around the woman's body as she arched her back against the pain. Other beings connected with birth and death hovered, ready to be of assistance. The child's head appeared and rotated. All the beings waited in silence as the woman screamed. And then came the final push.

The child slithered out and immediately the angel bent over the woman and cut the inner cord that passed from mother to child. The child's pattern became locked in its separateness at that moment, no longer integrated with that of the mother. The angel then stroked its fingers through the mother to rebalance her before turning to the child. As the other beings tended to the mother, the angel focused on the new life before it.

The child lay still and silent as the angel looked into its eyes. In the communion, the Angel sought the thread of the child's soul and when he found it, he tied a knot in it—a small delicate knot of remembrance. The child and the angel passed visions of recognition before the angel bent over and listened to the child whispering something on its first breath.

The angel then went to the mother and whispered in the mother's ear. He whispered the words spoken by the child; the Divine breath made word and the word was in flesh. The words traveled around the mother before settling deep in her heart. The words transformed themselves into sounds and joined with the mother's thoughts. They, together, became a name.

The mother bent over and whispered the child's name in her ear. And the angel withdrew.

CHAPTER 5

NOWHERE TO HIDE

The door clicked quietly as Benni tiptoed in, trying not to be heard. Her feet made no noise as she walked softly towards her room and fumbled for the doorknob. The tightness of her face relaxed from its grimace as soon as she was in the safety of her own room.

With a single click, the lamp flooded the room with light as she sat down on the edge of the bed. Her stomach lurched against its emptiness, but Benni knew that the tightness in her throat would never allow her to eat. Not that she wanted to eat anyway. All she wanted to do was to pull her hood deep over her head and just be there.

You are safe with us. Pull the hood deeper so that no one can see you. They all want to attack you, but we will keep you safe.

The voices reverberated around her head in a disco of comfort. Her fingers picked at her skin as she sat deciding whether or not to actually sleep tonight. She had begun to really hate sleep. Sleep meant a loss of control. Her new friends did not like her sleeping; they wanted her to hide in her hood and listen to them.

Her body stayed slumped, half propped up against the wall

with her hood pulled over her face. That was safe and warm. Slowly, she drifted into sleep.

A voice far far away called through her dream. Benni saw an open door and she could hear her mother calling through the door, but the voices told her not to trust anything. She hesitated in answering her mother but the calls became more and more urgent. Benni moved towards the door and her new friends screamed at her to run. The screams got louder and louder until Benni bolted in fear.

She sat up in bed panting with terror. They were right. Every time she fell asleep, something frightened her. It was much safer to not sleep. The dawn was rising, and Benni slid off the bed and padded into the kitchen.

The other girls, her housemates, would be up for work soon and Benni wanted to avoid them. They had all been best friends for so long, and had finally gotten their act together to rent a house. It was great fun all living together, until her new voices started to point things out to Benni. They showed her how the girls were always planning things behind her back, how they always told her lies and wanted to cheat her.

So Benni found it better to avoid them by getting up early and then hiding for the rest of the day. She had stopped going to work. Her colleagues just did not understand her needs any more. Only her new voices could be real to her. She bolted a cookie down with her tea and then scurried back into her room. She shut the door, pushed across the new chain and locked her dead bolt. Only then did she feel safe.

As always, she turned on her personal CD player and plugged herself into sound. The loud music that the new voices liked had been too abrasive for Benni at first, but now she was beginning to understand why they liked it so much. It pushed everything else out of her brain so there was no conflict anymore. No thoughts managed to filter through the music. That pleased the new friends. They always got angry if she questioned anything they said, or if any of her housemates challenged her about her change in lifestyle.

The music blasted through her brain, its strong fast rhythms strengthening the friends. She could feel that they liked it. It helped them to grow. She was happy that they were happy. Her head rocked back and forth as she played with the penknife and scratched their words on her skin.

Their poetry was so good that they wanted her to place it deep within her. Carving the words onto her skin was the best way to please them. The pain felt good. It was the only thing she could feel, and the feeling was strong. Just lately, everything had become numb, tasteless and bland. She did not hear the phone ring nor did she hear her housemates talk about her.

Her mother tried to be casual as she knocked on the door. Benni`s friends had rung her mother that morning, concerned that Benni was becoming ill. She needed to see for herself and she had sat all morning trying to justify intruding on her daughter's newfound independence. She had brought a bag of groceries for Benni, and she clung onto the paper bag as though it were an anchor.

It took a while for Benni to realize that someone was knocking at the door. Everyone had gone to work, and Benni drifted around the house like a scarf in the wind. The knock finally penetrated her brain and she slowly went to open the door.

As she saw her mother, the new friends began a torrent of warnings that her mother was out to harm her. Benni became deeply suspicious as her mother hugged her and handed her a large bag of groceries. She said she was shopping in the neighborhood and had thought of popping in.

Liar, liar

The new friends chanted through Benni`s brain,

Be careful, she will kill you.

The thought crept through Benni`s mind and she became doubly defensive.

Benni's mother wanted to cry out at the sad condition in which she found her daughter. Benni's face had sunken and dark rings circled her once curious eyes. *She must have lost about ten pounds*, thought her mother as her eyes wandered over the emaciated flesh.

Benni's eyes darted around the room as though watching for something. She would not communicate with her mother, but retreated under her sweater hood, backing away from her mother and looking for an escape route.

"Benni, you don't look well. Do you want to come and stay home for a few days, get yourself back on your feet?"

Benni's mother had thought that the suggestion would cheer Benni up. She always loved an excuse to go home for a few days and be waited on hand and foot. But Benni's mother had not anticipated the horrific change in her daughter. Benni backed away from her, visibly afraid.

"They were right, you are trying to kill me; you are all spying on me, all of you. Leave me alone, I just want to be alone!"

Benni threw a vase that she had grabbed. It smashed within inches of her mother's face. Her mother turned and ran. All the way home in the car she sobbed for her daughter, who was obviously in need of help.

Benni locked the door after her mother had run and then sat in the deafening silence afterwards. The hiss in the silence began to press against her skull, causing her to press her hands to her head in an effort to stop the pain and noise.

The friends began to chat to her and slowly she relaxed enough for them to continue feeding from her. As they fed from her energies and fear, a feeling of safety and well-being spread through her. She curled up in a ball and bathed in the false emotions that were filling her, and the parasites inched their way deeper and deeper into her being.

Benni's mother marched up and down her lounge floor with the phone stuck to her ear. She shouted and pleaded with the doctor to intervene with Benni and the doctor repeated his comment that nothing could be done without Benni`s consent. She slammed the phone down and kicked the table. Benni's father watched in silence as his wife worked herself into a frenzy of anger at a system that could not help her daughter. She stood looking out of the window in defeat, when an old woman walked past the house pushing a pram. A light dawned and she reached back for the phone with excitement.

"Hi, Grandmother. Greetings, I need your help..."

The old woman had been driven to the airport within the hour.

Benni had always loved her great-grandmother. The old woman was from the lost age of superstitions and mysteries. She had entranced Benni as a child with stories of her childhood in the mountains and sea towns of Turkey. If anyone could get through to Benni it was her.

Mina drove her grandmother to Benni`s house and was distraught when the old woman told her to drive off and not come back until she was called. She wanted to stay, to protect the old woman from Benni`s rage, and to try and reason with her daughter. But the old woman stood firm. She slowly climbed out of the car and hobbled her way up to the front door of the small house Benni now called home.

She did not knock, but just stood there, looking at the door. Mina set off slowly, watching in the rear-view mirror to ensure that the old woman was OK. She noticed that grandmother did not knock, but just stared.

Slowly, Benni opened the door. Mina was astounded. She drove off quietly, as requested, praying under her breath that her daughter could be convinced to see a doctor.

Benni felt something pierce through the fog in her mind. She had been wandering around her home, trying to find a place to settle, when sharpness had tapped on her head. It felt familiar and it was coming from the door. The voices tried to tell her not to go but the sharpness was louder than they were.

She opened her door and stood in shock as her beloved great-grandmother stood before her. The old woman bustled in before Benni could speak. The old woman turned on all the lights, pulled back all the curtains and then pulled Benni into her arms for a hug.

The girl felt an outpouring of something that felt good. The old woman grasped Benni's head and turned it this way and that, looking into her eyes, ears and mouth before turning her around and looking at her back. She then pulled out a scarf and tied it around Benni's neck.

A silence descended into Benni almost immediately. The voices stopped and the hissing lessened. Her eyes became heavy as her body realized that it had not slept properly in days.

The old woman steered her to the couch and told her to lie down while she used the phone. Benni did as she was told and lay on the couch. As she sank into its warmth, she could not remember this couch ever being so comfortable. Grandmother picked up the phone and called her granddaughter's cell phone.

"Come around now, we are taking her home."

Her mother appeared at the door a short while later and looked on the sleeping Benni in wonder. She looked up at her grandmother, who told her not to take anything of Benni's from here, that she must have no connections with what was in the house. Carefully, they awoke Benni and steered her towards the car. She moved like a drugged person and Mina asked her grandmother what she had given Benni to knock her out so heavily.

The old woman grinned, showing her gaps and gold teeth. "One of my scarves, little frog, one of my scarves."

Mina cringed at the old woman's use of her childhood nickname. The memory of grandmother's scarves came back in full technicolor. She remembered when she was a small child and her father was going off to war in Vietnam. Grandmother had given him a thin silk scarf. She had told him that while ever he wore that scarf, he would not be injured or captured. He returned from the war without a scratch on him despite being in the front line throughout his time in the forces.

Benni dozed all the way to her mother's house, feeling a warm comfort from being next to her great-grandmother. Her friends were shouting for her, but they seemed so far away, as if shouting from another street. Grandmother tapped her fingers on the back of the driver's seat, making Mina nervous.

"You will have to make this thing go faster; the scarf will wear off soon."

Mina screwed her face up in question as she looked at her grandmother through the rear mirror. She always thought that grandmother's scarves and their miracles would last for ages.

As though reading her thoughts, the grandmother told her that she could only hold the window into Benni open for a short time, just enough time for her to agree to the grandmother working on her.

Mina shot a look of panic at the old woman. She had thought that the scarf was being used to get Benni to a hospital. The old woman shook her head in sadness.

"There is nothing that any hospital can do for your daughter except to drug her. That would stop her reactions to what is going on. She would seem a little better, but really it will drive the Jinn deeper into her heart."

Benni lay dozing on her mother's bed while the adults argued it out in the kitchen below. Benni's father had hit the roof at the suggestion that his daughter was possessed. Mina herself was uneasy but she had seen some strange things in her time. Nearly all of them linked back to her grandmother.

The old woman clicked her teeth in impatience. She totally ignored Benni's father, acting as though he was not in the room. Instead, she looked at Mina. Mina knew deep in her heart that her grandmother was right, but she had heard scary things about people trying to cast out demons.

The old woman sat heavily down in the chair and rubbed her hands on the chair arms.

"Benni does not have demons, she has Jinn—a type of Jinn that has woken up with your modern age. It is attracted by the music, by the rhythms. It likes those fast rhythms. It likes the confusion and raw feelings of young people. It likes the sex and the drugs.

"It has a feast in your child, and you want to send her to a therapist. Psst! Rubbish, people! This country is a silly place full of silly people. Now you go to work, both of you. When you get back, if your daughter is not better, you take her to a therapist."

The old woman motioned with her head for them to go. The couple argued again before both agreeing to the bargain. This evening, they would call a therapist. With that, they left Benni sleeping while the old woman tottered around the house rearranging and moving things.

She decided to work in the lounge. The room was neutral, in the center, more or less, of the building, and it was not a sleeping room. This was the most important thing. She always remembered her own grandmother telling her never to do this work in a room where people slept: it would contaminate their souls, she had said.

She emptied her patched leather bag and pulled out five candles. She placed one in each direction, north, south, east, and west. She then placed one in the center of the room, putting it on a small table she had found. Her hands fumbled for the small box of matches and the silk pouch that was buried deep in the bottom of her bag.

Finally, she found the silk and she slowly drew it out. Her fingers pulled on the drawstring and opened the little pouch, spilling out the contents. A small golden icon on a chain rolled into her palm. She held it up and looked at the black face of the Blessed Virgin of Ephesus.

This face always made her heart contract. She had left her home village on the outskirts of Ephesus when she was a young woman heavy with her first child. Her old stiff hands touched the icon with reverence before placing it to her forehead and then lips.

The icon fitted into a thick chain, which the old woman strung around her neck before tottering off into the kitchen in search of salt and water. The bowls were laid out neatly, one full of water, and one full of salt. She prayed first over the water, then the salt, before pouring the salt into the water and stirring it with her finger. She bent over and whispered prayers over the surface of the water as she stirred, asking God the Father, and then the Mother of God, to work with her.

Her hands carried the bowl carefully back to the circle she had created and she placed it gently in the north. One by one, she went to the candles, starting in the center and then working clockwise around the directions starting in the north. She lit each candle, stood silently before the candle and asked that the saint of that direction be with her in her work. Once she was happy with what she had done, she stood by the center candle, feeling the peace and calmness that had crept into the room.

She prayed silently for the strength to do what she was about to do. She had only ever done this three times in her life before and each time it had brought her to her knees with exhaustion and terror. Her own grandmother had taught her this, and she in her own turn had added some Christian aspects to it to make it more compatible with the world in which she now lived.

Her eyes scanned the room for one last check before she decided it was finally time to work on Benni. Her breath labored as she slowly climbed the stairs to the bedroom. She could hear Benni`s snores before she got to the room.

Benni lay peacefully lapping up the sleep that had evaded her for days, and Grandmother stood looking around the room. She could feel them in the room with Benni and she could feel their panic as they realized their grip was being loosened.

Benni needed shaking a few times before she finally surfaced from the grogginess that surrounded her. The old woman frowned as she watched the young girl struggle to surface. Benni slowly opened her eyes and smiled as the grandmother stroked her head. Grandmother told her that she would need some work done on her because her soul had become weakened and needed help.

Benni smiled at the old woman. She always had memories of her favorite granny telling her weird stuff, and here she was again, trying to frighten her with silly stories. But what the heck? She decided to agree, just for the laugh of it.

The voices were so distant that they had become a low mumbling in the background. Grandmother could hear them too, every time she got close to Benni. But she knew that she did not have much time, for the effect of the scarf was already fading.

Benni followed the old woman down the stairs and into the lounge. Benni`s eyebrows rose as high as they would go when she saw the candles lit around the room. Something within her panicked, but she ignored it. She lay down where grandmother told her and got herself comfortable.

Starting in the north, the old woman silently communed before the flame in each direction, again asking the saints and powers to be with her in her work. She felt the contact of each power reach out to her as she processed around the directions. When she came back to the center, she bent over and took the scarf from around Benni's neck.

Instantly, the noise became unbearable to Benni. The voices returned in shouts and screams and Benni placed her hands to her ears. Grandmother carried on regardless. She sprinkled the salted water around the room and anointed Benni on the head, eyes, ears, heart and abdomen. The noise lessened and Benni began to relax. The old woman struggled to sit on the floor at the head of her granddaughter, adjusting cushions and rugs until she was in a position that she could comfortably stay in for a while. She told Benni to rest and close her eyes, to go to sleep if she wanted.

Benni tried hard to hear what her voices were saying as their tone faded into the distance. She was beginning to feel lonely and afraid, as one by one the voices turned back to whispers.

The grandmother closed her eyes and sat quietly. She knew that the parasite beings that had latched onto Benni were powerful and that ceremony alone would not work; she would have to use her mind and go in vision to help Benni effectively.

Instead of confronting the beings head on, she decided to work primarily on Benni, tuning her, cleansing and strengthening her so that the beings could not hold on to her so well.

Using her inner vision, she saw herself in the room with Benni. She stood up and walked to the girl, placed her hand inside Benni`s body. She called to Benni, and slowly the inner body that housed the soul edged its way out of the physical body. Benni stood before her looking weak and pale. Other beings tried to come out too, but grandmother shoved them back in. In one swift movement, she picked Benni up and walked to the central flame. The flame fell down a well that had opened up beneath it and grandmother, holding Benni, followed.

They fell and fell, down through the underworld, passing through the realm of ancestors, the realm of faeries and the realm of the Titans. The grandmother became more and more of her ageless self as she fell, allowing the burden of old age to fall from her as she tumbled through the Underworld.

A light appeared below them and they fell towards the light. They emerged in a large cavern that had a rough-hewn entrance in each of the four directions. Each entrance was draped with a curtain of fabric that moved gently with a breeze. In the center of the cave was a strange standing stone that grandmother approached and touched reverently: the stone at the center of all things.

A noise came from the north and Grandmother turned to see an old woman appear from behind the curtain. She beckoned for the grandmother to bring Benni and to follow her. They wove their way through strange low-roofed passage-ways covered in wall paintings. Strange demon faces peered through the darkness, their faces painted in dazzling colors that appeared in the instant of the flame torchlight before vanishing back into the darkness.

Benni had all but collapsed in Grandmother's arms by the time they surfaced in a small circular cavern with a stone bed in the center. Below the bed was a well that vanished down into the blackness. Two more old women emerged, their long white hair wrapped and woven into cloaks that covered their bodies. They motioned for the grandmother to place Benni on the stone bed and then stand back.

She hid in the shadows of the cave while the three old women peered at the young girl. They started to circle the bed, humming and clicking their fingers as they went. Their feet moved faster, turning around the directions as they circled the bed.

The noise of the humming seemed to embed itself in the fabric of the cave and Grandmother became afraid. The hair of the old women loosened from its weave and began to fly though the air as they turned. Many strands of the gray and white hair became interlocked until a beautiful web pattern of hair emerged over the women as they turned.

A wind generated from the center of the turning and began to howl around the cave. It became more powerful as each second passed, growing into a tornado that encased the bed, the women, and the young girl.

Grandmother watched Benni in terror as the wind pulled on the girl's skin; Benni`s skin began to shear away in the wind.

Her fragile skin and hair flew up into the whirlwind as the muscle fiber began to strain from its foundation. That, too, whipped up into the air, turning around the directions before vanishing. Then came the organs. One by one they were torn from the girl's body and vanished into the chaos until all that was left were the bones. The noise of the bones cracking and splintering drove itself into the grandmother's heart as she covered her eyes from the horror that she witnessed.

Once the bones had gone, all that was left was the outline of a human shape that fell away to reveal a pattern. It was a single thread of an unbalanced jagged shape. The three women grasped the shape and pulled hard. The line straightened, causing an explosion that tore through the canopy of woven hair that belonged to the women. Grandmother watched as the eternal essence of Benni was thrown to the four winds.

Benni had fallen into a deep sleep, finding herself whirling and swirling in a wind that cleansed her soul. She reveled in the cleansing until she heard the scream of a terrible wind. She wanted to run, but her legs would not work. She wanted to crouch up and cover her head, but she was frozen and could not move so much as a finger. Benni was convinced that she was about to die.

What followed came so quickly that she could not prepare for it. The wind blew through her, tearing her to pieces until nothing was left. All that remained were thought and feeling. Benni was finally free of the compression of a body.

Her consciousness passed through the rock and earth as she emerged from the underworld. Her thoughts spread out across the face of the land and Benni merged with the trees and the plants. Moving through them, she felt their waiting in time, their power as it passed through the ages. The emotions of the flowers streamed all around her, flowing through her in blessing as she communed with the entirety of nature. The animals joined with her, and the divinity within substance touched her as she passed through cities, towns, desert, and ocean.

Her soul melted within the substance of being and Benni felt as if she were part of a single creature that made up the whole universe.

A sound traveled through time and Benni tried to turn from it. But the sound got louder and more insistent. She was drawn towards it against her will and Benni fought back. She did not want to go towards the sound; she wanted to stay within all things.

Finally, the sound hooked into her and drew her at great speed through time, substance and being, until she passed through the rock and back into the Underworld.

In the deep cave, the sisters stood immobile in silence, holding the thin thread that was Benni. One of the old women put her head back and cried out a sound that shook its way through Grandmother's soul. The sound caused a shock wave that spread out through the land and reverberated all around them. The thin line moved and became a wavy line that had a beauty and harmony all of its own.

A call came back, and the old women began to turn—this time in the opposite direction. As they turned faster, the wavy line became thickened and deeper in its harmonic shape.

Bones started to appear, along with organs, muscle and flesh. Skin covered the flesh until finally Benni began to reappear.

The whirlwind lessened and grandmother stood up as the old women came to a halt. Benni lay in total balance, her soul shining out from the renewed body.

The old women motioned for the grandmother to pick Benni up. The grandmother looked around her for the entrance and prepared to take Benni back up to the surface world. But one of the women grabbed grandmother's arm.

"No, she is not finished yet. Her soul has been re-harmonized, but there is damage in the etheric body and the physical body. We cannot help with that; it is not what we do. You must take her up there and they will help you."

The old woman pointed to a stairway that vanished up into the darkness. The two other women stood nodding their heads and smiling at grandmother as she looked around in panic.

She was tired; she did not know if she had the strength to stay in vision and carry out the next task. But as she looked upon her great-grandchild lying in her arms, she knew that she had no choice, even if it killed her. She had lived her life and was a grand old age. She was seventy-nine, and yet Benni still had all of her life in front of her. Yes, she would find the strength somehow.

Slowly, she climbed the stairs and left the cave of the old women behind her. The stairway was dark, and Grandmother had to walk carefully, feeling her way with her feet as she ascended into a mystery. A dim light up ahead beckoned her and Grandmother panted under the strain of carrying Benni.

She emerged in a large underworld temple that lay under a blanket of dust and neglect. The old woman wandered among the columns, looking in awe at the strange carved faces that stared at her as she processed past. At the far end of the temple, a statue emerged out of the darkness as the grandmother drew closer.

She looked on in awe as she drew closer to the image, which caused every cell in her being to panic. Out of the darkness stared an image of a woman, half lioness and half human. The image seemed so large that it vanished up into the darkness, only her red eyes flashed through the shadows as if lit by a light all of their own.

The Goddess was seated, and between her feet was a carved door that opened slowly. At the feet of this ancient Goddess was a stone bed and grandmother instinctively laid Benni on the bed and stepped back in fear.

A man and a woman emerged from the doorway and greeted Grandmother with respect. They looked at Benni and then back at the grandmother.

"You must not be afraid; please, be with us while we heal this child."

Their voices seemed to speak within the grandmother's head and the old woman nodded. Her hand instinctively went to the icon around her throat and the young man smiled.

"The Blessed Virgin is beloved here also."

His words helped the grandmother to relax as she watched the strange woman slowly walk around the stone bed that held the sleeping Benni.

Stopping, the woman peered at Benni closely before reaching into her and drawing out something. The man worked with her and together, they delved into Benni, taking out things which did not belong there. They replaced certain organs before stroking her hair and bathing her skin. Finally, they both placed their hands on her. Grandmother watched as light poured from the couple into Benni. Benni seemed to grow in size and strength, her skin glowing from the energy that was being passed into her.

The couple withdrew and motioned for the grandmother to pick up the young girl. They pointed to a stairway at the back of the statue. Grandmother looked up at the Goddess figure before scooping up Benni. She did not know who or what the statue represented, but she wanted to say thank you. Her lips moved silently as she moved towards the stone stairs.

Again, she climbed, her back hurting and her head ringing from the strain of staying in vision so long while carrying the soul of another being. She began to pray to the Blessed Virgin as she slowly placed one foot in front of the other.

They emerged in yet another cavern. But this one was small with a round pool of dark water in the center. Steam from the water filled the room as Grandmother strained to see in the strange light that filtered out from the rocks. A voice called her through the mist and grandmother stiffened. Again, her name filtered through the damp air and Grandmother moved towards the voice.

She found a bed of ferns and laid Benni upon it. The water steamed, inviting Grandmother to bathe in it with its soft heat and peaceful stillness. Slowly, she peeled off her clothing and slid into the water, letting out a cry of pleasure as the water closed around her. The water cleansed and renewed her. Every cell in her body responded by renewing and awakening to the gift of the deep pool. Again, she heard her name called, softly, like a whisper.

She stood up in the water just in time to see a woman half concealed by the shadows. The woman beckoned her to come out of the pool and Grandmother climbed out with a strength she had not felt in decades. She dripped on the side of the pool, and was trying to wring her hair out when she noticed a robe near her feet. The woman motioned for her to put it on.

Its fabric melted into the grandmother's skin, fusing with her and becoming one with the old woman. She looked at herself in astonishment as she felt the fabric become like a barrier or protection that covered her from head to toe.

The woman stepped out of the shadows and Grandmother was instantly filled with fear. The woman who stood before her had skin of tree bark, the eyes of an animal, and hair that seemed to grow into the ground, like roots. Her hands were very old and yet her face was young. There was something about this woman, this being, which made Grandmother's heart sing for joy even through the terror.

The woman held out her hand to the grandmother. Grandmother knew she was asking for a gift. She did not know what to give. Without thinking, she took the icon from around her neck and gave it to the woman. The woman looked at the icon and then covered it with her hands.

The icon vanished and what replaced it was a pearl. She held the pearl to the old woman's lips and the grandmother swallowed it. As she swallowed the pearl, the woman before her started to change. She took on the form of the Virgin in the icon and Grandmother put her arms up to cover her eyes.

The woman reached out and touched Grandmother, carefully pulling her arms away from her face. She smiled and touched the grandmother's cheek.

You have loved me all your life, and now you cower from me?

The grandmother was confused. She did not understand what was happening. All she knew was that she had to heal her great-grandchild. The woman caught Grandmother's thoughts and looked at Benni.

Leave her with me, you must go to the surface world and clean the body. Here are your tools and here is your guide.

The woman handed the grandmother a box of tools and a strange being that appeared to be half- crab and half-human appeared at her side.

Together, they climbed the stairs to the outside world, emerging back in the lounge where Grandmother had first started. Grandmother looked at Benni's body as it lay sleeping on the floor. When she looked closer, she began to see things moving within Benni.

Grandmother's hands moved as if guided. She slowly

opened Benni's body up like a box and peered inside. Many strange insect-like creatures scurried around, and Grandmother reached for the toolbox. In it, she found a small hand-held vacuum. She vacuumed out Benni's body, careful to look in each corner. Opening the toolbox, she found a hosepipe, and began to squirt water in the body to cleanse it. Dirt and debris tumbled out on the water and splashed on the grandmother.

The crab moved around to Benni's side and moved quickly with its hands and claws. It started to withdraw something from Benni's womb and Grandmother joined in to help. Grandmother felt something move under her touch. She grabbed it and started to pull. Whatever she was pulling tried to pull back and its strength terrified Grandmother. Inch by inch, they pulled out a strange octopus-like being with many tentacles reaching deep into every corner of Benni's body. The crab-being grabbed the parasite and jumped down into the underworld with it firmly in its grasp.

Grandmother peered and poked until she was sure there was not much left in the body. She sat back on her heels and looked at Benni's body. Something did not look right. She looked closer and saw that the body looked slightly out of focus. She ran her hands over the body and it felt like it was out of focus.

Carefully, she placed her hands on Benni's head and again, felt the strangeness. It was almost as if there were two bodies in one. She could feel what was Benni, but she could feel something else. She grabbed the something else and began to pull. A loud shrieking noise emitted from the body as she pulled out what looked like a two-dimensional carbon copy of Benni's body.

When it was finally out, it moved on its own. Grandmother was afraid. She put her foot on it to keep it still while she closed up the body and put her tools back in her bag. The thing did not seem to have much strength and Grandmother looked curiously at it as it wriggled under her foot.

She grabbed it and held on tight as she copied the crabbeing and jumped down into the cave. The carbon copy began to grow as they fell. They landed softly beside the pool in the cave, and Grandmother drew away in horror as she looked at this tall, insect-like being screaming beside her.

A noise came from the pool and the insect was drawn to the water. It leaned over the pool and Grandmother, acting on instinct, knocked it into the pool. It vanished into the darkness and the cave became silent again.

Grandmother looked for Benni but could see nothing until a light grew brighter on the opposite side of the pool. Women emerged from the darkness and one by one filled the cave. The light poured out of them, lighting the underworld cavern with a mystical light brighter than the sun. They gathered around the grandmother, stroking her hair and singing to her as she frantically called out for Benni.

A horn sounded. From a crack in the cave wall stepped a vision that would stay with the grandmother through the last of her years and would light her way in death. A woman clothed in stars that glowed like the sun stepped from the rock and stood by the pool. Her hair cascaded in a thick cloak to the floor and at her feet shone the moon.

Grandmother bowed her head at the vision before her. She knew who this was. Miriam, Star of the Sea, the blessed virgin Mother of God. From among the strands of her hair emerged Benni looking strong and healthy.

In silence Benni walked to the grandmother, who took her by the hand. A silent communion between Grandmother and the Goddess passed before the old woman turned and led Benni up a stone spiral stairway that ascended to the surface world. The Grandmother struggled as she tried to hold the vision long enough to get Benni back in her body, counting each step that she took in an effort to concentrate her thoughts and not collapse.

They emerged together in the lounge and Grandmother guided Benni back into the body that had been cleansed and prepared. Opening her eyes, she fingered the icon that was around her neck, the icon she had given to the Goddess in gift. Struggling to get up, she got to her knees and then stood, in pain, holding the icon and chain in her hand.

Going first to the north, she stood before the candle and held the icon out. Under her breath, she asked the powers of that direction to place whatever was necessary for Benni's protection into the icon. The request was repeated in each direction until she got to the central flame. The flame held steady as she held the icon before the flame and whispered so that Benni would not hear.

"Lord God, Father of the heavens above, great Goddess, Mother of the earth below my feet, grant that this image will be a window of your divine power."

Benni stirred from the deep sleep that had overtaken her. The Grandmother blew out the candles one by one, sending the flames back into the Void as Benni opened her eyes and looked around. She placed the sacred icon around Benni's neck and stroked her hair.

"Come, you need good food, put some meat on them bones."

Grandmother steered Benni into the kitchen for one of her famous garlic omelets. She watched her great-granddaughter as the young girl tucked into the food. When she had finished, she pushed the plates over to one side.

"So, Benni, talk to me. How do you feel and how did you get in such a mess in the first place?"

The Grandmother's eyes were like a hawk as she watched the girl. She could see that the girl had cleared; she was right that Benni was not in need of a doctor. If Benni had needed a doctor, the scarf and the vision would have had little or no effect on her.

Benni looked a little shell-shocked. "I feel...I feel as if I have been living with a talking blanket over my head for so long. It's difficult to explain. But I feel clear and wonderful now. What did you do? What was wrong with me?"

The old woman peeled an apple as she listened to Benni.

"I have cleaned you. But you will be weak for a while. You will need to stay here, and I will too, just for a few days until your energy is solid. It happens. Who knows what causes it—strange friends, drugs, sex, anything. It's like catching hair lice, it just needs cleaning up. Sometimes it's an illness that needs a doctor. But I could see from your eyes that it was not a doctor you needed. You need to rest, eat, sleep and be simple. OK?"

Benni nodded and chewed on the apple. The old woman got up slowly, trying desperately hard not to let Benni know the toll that the work had taken on her. She would need to rest for a long while.

"Now mind you don't take off the icon I gave you. It is very precious to me, from my childhood. It will keep you safe, just as it kept me safe."

CHAPTER 6

THE RIVER OF GENERATIONS

Connie slammed the door shut in her mother's face and hoped that her violent words had hurt the older woman. The bedroom door vibrated with the blow, causing flakes of paint to fall off and drift down to Connie's feet. Silence followed. Connie strained to listen and smiled as she heard her mother's quiet footsteps slowly retreat from the battleground.

Later, as she heard her mother weeping, Connie felt the closed grip of guilt pulling at her throat. She wanted to leap out of bed and hold her mother, whispering to her that she would never leave her; she would always be here for her. But she knew that was silly. She had to leave. College was about to start, and she had to fly the nest if she wanted any sort of independent life.

Maria, Connie's mother, had pleaded with Connie not to go to college. The doctor had told Connie that there was no pill on God's earth that was going to help her mother's deep depressions and that her fear of losing Connie was a deep-seated childhood fear. It had to be. What other explanation was there?

Connie had tried everything to loosen her mother's grip,

but the fear had only gotten stronger in the older woman, causing Connie to despair. In a last-ditch attempt at freedom, she had tried hard to make her mother hate her, but all it had achieved was a feeling of hatred within Connie for herself.

The ceiling that she had stared at for the last seventeen years hovered over her like some giant foot about to squash her. She had always loved her room with its little cottage windows and strange twisted walls. Connie loved old buildings and this eighteenth-century moorland cottage buried deep in the heart of north Yorkshire was the center of her heart. Or it had been until just recently.

Now the familiar rickety old floor, the bed that squealed when she lay on it and the chest of drawers with eyes instead of handles all crowded in on her. Was this to be her prison? Was she to be trapped here for as long as her mother lived? Why was her mother like this anyway?

Connie realized, as she lay there pulling threads out of an old knitted blanket, that she knew virtually nothing about her mother and her family. Her father had died when she was little, and Connie seemed to have always lived in a vacuum. It had never bothered her until today. All she knew was that her great-grandmother had come here from somewhere else and no one talked about her. Grandmother, too, was a mystery. The local villagers would say, "Ah yes, Granny Beckett; hmm, yes." And that was it. Any further questions would be met with a shrug of the shoulders.

The following morning, Connie decided to walk on the moors to get away from the house for a while and think. The moors were a special place for Connie. She breathed deeply as she wove her way through the bracken and heather, savoring the scent of the peat and the tiny heather flowers.

Moorland had its very own sound. A curlew in flight or the scurry of a hare would occasionally puncture the dense silence. Her hands rested on her hips as she stopped to drink in the view. A vast carpet of purple stretched out before her, peppered with limestone outcrop and in the distance, the cross. She would aim for the cross today. It was a large wooden structure set in concrete designed to guide anyone lost on the moors.

Connie had been born and raised here. She knew each tuft of grass, each sheep and each sparrow hawk. She would be able to find her way home blindfolded, just by the different scents that shifted around the landscape: heather here, bracken there, and sheep to your left and heavy peat by the center. But most visitors got lost. Some died when the mist descended, dropping the temperature and trapping them into an impenetrable darkness.

Connie knew better than to try to walk home if a mist came down. So she always carried her backpack, her moors pack, lest the darkness should sweep over her. It had happened many times, and she would just wait it out.

The sky was beautiful: full of skylarks reaching for the stars, calling to her as she ventured over the rough terrain. Heather brushed against her legs as she walked, perfuming her with the essence of moorland. Sheep grunted as she walked past. Rabbits darted this way and that as they heard the footfall of humanity drawing closer.

This is where her heart sang. This was her freedom, she thought to herself as she reached the cross. Slowly, she slid down the concrete, her back to the cross and her knees bent. Her stomach rumbled as she opened the bag. She did not notice the clouds gathering as she opened up her sandwiches, nor did she notice the drop in temperature as the sheep ambled discreetly over to her, sniffing at her delicious food.

The sheep tried to pretend that they were not interested in her, edging nearer all the time as they pulled on the sparse grazing. The temptation became too much for one youngster who trotted straight up to Connie and demanded food. His soft eyes pleaded for some of her salad sandwich and Connie could not resist. They munched together, Connie deep in thought and sheep deep in pleasure.

It was not until the characteristic roll of mist lapped at her feet that she realized what was happening. All around her, the faces of cold sheep loomed out of the mist as the damp dark killer stalked the moors once again. She did not have time for this and yet she was too far out on the moor to safely get back. Although she knew the way, the mist was disorientating and the moorland was riddled with pothole entrances, some hundreds of feet deep.

She pulled her moors pack towards her and emptied it out on the ground. A plastic fertilizer bag curled out along with her thermal hat, plastic hooded jacket and gloves. She placed the water bottle and mint cake back in the bag and tied it up well so that the sheep would not be able to help themselves. Connie then did what she always did in mist. She wrapped herself up, put on her hat and gloves, slid into the fertilizer bag up to her neck, and waited.

The silence of the mist was stronger than the general quiet of the moors. And with the silence always came fear. It rode in with the moisture, weaving its way around every living thing as the moorland held its breath, waiting for the return of the sun. Connie needed a diversion. She thought of her mother and the black moods of deep despair that crept upon her without reason, like the moor mist.

Connie's mind began to wander, and she began to daydream. Closing her eyes against the wall of invisibility, she was pulled into sleep. Almost immediately she found herself wandering through the mist in her dream.

At that point, a face passed through the mist and stared beyond Connie. Connie turned around to see what the face was looking at. She knew she was dreaming, but the dream felt strange. She could still hear the snuffles of the sheep nearby as they hung around her for safety, and yet she knew she was deeply asleep.

Her eyes strained through the mist just in time to see the back of someone vanish. Curiosity overwhelmed Connie as she decided to follow. Her feet seemed much more confident than she did as she walked briskly over the clumps of heather in an attempt to keep up. The back of the mystery person seemed familiar somehow, and yet she could not quite place who it was.

The terrain began to change, and Connie became confused. She found herself pushing past bushes and trees. And yet she knew without doubt that there were no bushes or trees on this moor. Voices drifted through the clearing mist and Connie became startled as she heard her mother's name mentioned. The undergrowth obscured the scene ahead as she pushed through the trees in an attempt to find the voice and the mystery person whom she had been following.

Connie emerged from the trees and stopped short, not moving another inch. Before her was a woman holding a child and weeping as though her heart would break. Carefully, the woman cupped the face of the small silent child and kissed her with such emotion that Connie had to look away. The sobs lodged in Connie's throat as she struggled to stay silent. It was obvious to Connie that this woman was saying a final farewell to her beloved daughter.

Behind the child stood a man and an older woman, both glowering at the weeping woman. Their clothing looked strange to Connie, as though they were from the past and yet, in the dream, it all seemed normal.

The child stood expressionless. She stared beyond the weeping woman as though trying to lock herself out of the situation. The man moved forward and knocked the woman away from the child with one sweeping blow.

"Get away from her, you have no right to be with her. Your people could not mother a cow, let alone a child. Be away with you and never come near this village again. If you do, I will kill you. Go."

Connie moved closer to let herself be seen. She wanted to intervene, but she was not sure what to do. She looked to the child who looked back at Connie. Her eyes were so familiar to Connie, so close to her somehow. The woman stepped back and stood upright. Her face, as Connie could now see, was badly bruised and cut.

The situation began to sink into Connie. This was mother and child, and the father was taking the child away from her mother. The child was to be handed to the paternal grandmother who stood silently in the corner. Connie wanted to stop this right now. Her mind moved forward to challenge the man, but her body did not follow. She was rooted to the spot. She called out to the mother who by now was walking off, weeping into her hands. But Connie's voice was silent; no sound could pass her lips.

The man picked up the child, who was still silent and staring. He turned with the old woman and vanished into the mist. Connie's feet became unstuck and she followed the mother into the mist, calling for her to stop and wait. But the woman did not hear as she stumbled crying through the woods.

The trees grew thicker and dense until Connie had to push her way through the undergrowth. Her breath became heavy from the exertion as she fought her way forward. How had the woman managed to move so quickly through all this? Connie's thoughts tumbled around her mind as she ploughed on. Why were they dressed so strangely? She knew she was still dreaming, she could feel herself asleep. And yet something within her knew that what she had seen was real.

The overgrowth began to ease off and the sound of a woman singing lullabies drifted through the thinning mist. Connie could not see her, but she could smell wood smoke and hear the crackle of a fire. The trees began to part, and Connie stood behind a bush to observe unseen.

A small campfire gave off aromatic peat smoke and a woman sat beside it. She was dressed in rags and shawls of exotic design and color. Her long dark hair was matted in places and hung lifelessly around her white, heavily-lined face. Every time she moved, a loud noise came from the rows of metal bangles that slid back and forth, up and down her thin arms. She was lifting something to her mouth to drink. Connie edged nearer to see what it was.

Wood smoke blew her way and Connie's eyes began to sting badly as she strained to see. The woman held a bottle up to her mouth but missed. Some of the liquid dribbled down her dress and the wind blew the scent towards Connie. Alcohol. The woman was making herself drunk. The lullaby began again, and the strange woman started to rock as she sang. Connie recognized the song as one her mother had sung to her as a child. It was in a strange language and Connie had always assumed it was a language that her mother had made up.

The woman began to sob as she sang. The pain and sorrow that flooded from the woman washed over Connie, awakening her own sad memories as she stood in silence. She had to do something, anything. The impulse allowed her to move forward, and Connie walked up to the woman, slowly, so as not to startle her.

The woman did not seem to notice Connie. She had stopped singing but was muttering to herself. "My babies, my babies."

The words were repeated over and over as she cried. Connie wanted to cry too. The impulse broke through, and Connie sat at the side of the woman and began to cry. All the frustration with her own mother, all the deep sadness that had always haunted her from God knows where surfaced and left her as she wept.

The woman became silent and listened. She could hear the sound of weeping. Her head nodded. "So, the spirits cry with me, I have not been abandoned."

The woman looked into the fire and poked it with a stick as she wiped her eyes. Connie was shocked. The woman obviously could not see her, but she could hear her. Her mind began to race. Maybe if she could communicate with this woman, she could help her.

"Can you hear me, old woman?" Connie had an idea.

The old woman drew her shawl nearer to herself and nodded. "Yes, I hear you, spirit of the forest. Bless you for being here."

Connie took a minute to think about what she was going to do. She had to do something to help this woman, and her mother had always told her that talking helps. She edged a little closer to the woman and looked into her eyes. "Tell me about your pain, that I might share it with you."

The old woman smiled sadly, showing her lack of teeth. Her tears fell again as she looked back at the fire. "It is the curse of my own people. I left my people for the love of a man." The woman paused to spit on the ground.

"I had children. When he grew tired of me, he took my children away from me. He took all my babies. Some of them died without me there to care for them. My eldest daughter Margarita was married off to a good family. She had a child, Maria. Margarita wanted to return to the old ways, to the ways of my family, the Romani people."

"Her husband took Maria and beat my daughter to death in front of her child. This world is a wicked place, so I must leave it. I have left nothing behind. No one has survived who will honor me or remember me. I will wander the earth forever with my pain because no one will ever remember my sorrow and share it with me."

Connie sat silently for a moment, trying to digest what had

just been revealed to her. Now she knew why the silent child in the forest was so familiar to her. It was her mother! And this poor old woman was her great-grandmother. Pain and fear had cascaded down through her family for reasons, till now, unknown to Connie. But now it was very clear to her, and she knew what she must do.

She laid a hand on the back of the old woman, who did not seem to feel the touch. Grandmother, listen to me. I know of the future and what it holds for your line. They will not forget you and you will be honored for generations to come. I will ensure that your sorrows are recounted and shared, and that your name is respected."

Connie wanted to tell the old woman who she was, but something within her stopped her. The old woman began to cry again, but this time with a feeling of relief in her tears.

A drained feeling began to creep up on Connie and she wanted to sleep. And yet she was asleep. The old woman too seemed suddenly weary. Her hair fell around her as she lay down by the fire. The wind blew dried leaves around her slumped body and the fire died down as the night cold took the strength from the flames.

Quietly, almost respectfully, the mist crept in and engulfed the old woman as she slept. Connie knew deep within her that the old woman had lain down to die, at peace in her mind that she would not be forgotten.

Connie thought about what the woman had told her, and it all began to finally make sense to her. That was why her mother held such fear and sadness within her. She was always terrified of someone leaving her. Connie hung her head in shame as she remembered the hurtful words she had inflicted on her mother. For three generations the women and children had been torn from each other, and worst of all, Maria had seen her own mother killed before her. Connie wondered if her mother remembered that terrible event.

The sleepiness dragged her deeper and deeper down until she fell into blackness. Warmth comforted her as she rested in the darkness and Connie sighed a long, drawn-out sigh, releasing tension that had built up for many years.

It was the nose of the curious sheep that startled Connie into waking. She opened her eyes to a nose exploring the scent of food around her mouth. Connie shood the creature away and sat up to stretch. The mist was clearing, and Connie slowly climbed out from her fertilizer bag, stretched her damp limbs and shook off the cold. The dream had faded into the back of her memory, simmering there until the right time, sometime, to surface.

On the way back to the house, something had lightened her step. Maybe it was a good deep sleep or the fresh air perhaps? Whatever it was, Connie felt renewed and ready for the next round of conflict with her mother. She groaned internally as she approached the cottage and saw her mother sitting outside in the sun with the village Granny busybody. Obviously, her mother was recruiting the villagers to persuade Connie not to leave and go to college.

Conflict was not what she wanted but Connie prepared herself. What she heard made her stop in her tracks and stare at her mother. Mrs. 'Busybody-Know-It-All' looked up at Connie's face and smiled a huge smile. "I hear you are going to college in a few weeks. Congratulations, your mother is very proud of you." Connie could not speak, so she just nodded and looked to her mother for an explanation.

Later, as they sat by the fire, Connie waited for her mother to talk about her change of heart. Instead of the usual frantic knitting that her mother did whenever she had nothing else to do, Connie's mother sat quietly with her hands in her lap. Her voice was low and peaceful as she spoke.

"Today, while you were out, I sat on the edge of the moor, you know, on the old codgers' seat, and I looked at the view over the valley. Maybe I'm just stupid, but it has never struck me before how beautiful the world out there is. And that keeping you here is stopping you from being a part of all that."

The older woman fell silent and looked at her hands. Connie could see it was very difficult for her mother and that this was her mother's way of trying to let go. The young woman knelt beside her mother and tentatively placed a hand on her arm. Physical contact was not something Connie was used to. They had always maintained a distant relationship.

"Mum, I'm not going away forever. I want to return here and work in the local clinic. To do that though, I have to get my degree, so I have to be away. There will be school breaks. I don't really want to leave you. But this is the only way that I can really stay in the village in the long term."

Connie fell silent. She had never before mentioned coming back to work in the village. She had never even thought about it until it popped out of her mouth. It was at that point that she realized that she wanted her children to grow up here, perched on the edge of the moors among the sheep and the elders. She wanted her children to be rooted, to be loved and to be safe with her. Connie also wanted her children to have their grandmother close and to be part of a solid community.

That night, Connie dreamed of the mist on the moors. Out of the mist drifted a lullaby and as Connie reached forward to see who was singing, she came across a little girl sitting cross-legged by the style, singing at the top of her voice. Connie recognized the little girl from somewhere deep in her memory. Connie asked her who she was and what she was doing.

"Oh, my name is Maria and I'm just waiting for my best friend to come home again. I'm singing so that she will not lose her way."

CHAPTER 7
A RAVEN'S TALE

ENGLAND, 1985

The yearling trotted up the field, his tail held high with pride as he tossed his head, copying the stallion in the next field. He then put his head down and galloped at top speed from one side of the field to the other. He was a champion, he was invincible, he was...super horse!

He came to a full stop and stood by the gate panting. Being a super horse made him very hungry, and he could have sworn that he heard the clink of the feed bucket coming up the yard to the field gate.

Sure enough, around the corner came Agnes, whistling at the top of her voice and pretending not to see Pony. They could not think of a name for him when he was born, so they all called him Pony. Pony liked this game of not seeing. Agnes would walk past him, climb over the fence and stand in the middle of the field. She would then call for Pony and Pony would whinny from behind her. She would turn around, pretending not to be able to see him and he would have to trot up behind her and nudge her bottom.

The stallion stood and watched this performance, for the umpteenth time wondering what on earth they were doing. He could not understand why that young fledgling son of his did not dive straight for the bucket and stick his head in it as soon as he saw it. Was he nuts?

Agnes laughed as she was butted in the bottom. She turned around to pull Pony's ears, which he loved, before holding out the bucket of alfalfa for him. Pony vanished into the bucket of bliss, making lots of happy eating noises and surfacing occasionally to shake his head up and down as he chewed: it made the food taste better. Once he had emptied the bucket, then came the treat. Agnes looked around first to make sure that her father did not see her.

When she was sure all was clear, she pulled out a packet of Polo mints, the ultimate British horse food, or so Pony thought. She slowly opened the wrapping. Pony hopped from hoof to hoof. She carefully peeled back the silver paper. Pony tried to tell her how to do it by whinnying softly and shaking his head quickly.

She put her finger into the tube of mints. Pony pawed the ground in anticipation. It was killing him. His top lip started to search for the mint among her fingers until he finally found one. He jerked his head back in pleasure, looking at Agnes with bright intelligent eyes. She held out her hand, as she always did, and Pony, careful not to knock the mint from her hand, scooped up the holed mint delight and rolled it to his teeth where it was munched with great appreciation.

Pony was a happy Pony. Agnes was a happy Agnes. The stallion was not a happy stallion because no one ever gave him Polo mints, no matter how hard he thought at people. And that was what he was doing now: thinking at Agnes. Agnes picked up the thought immediately.

Want Polo mints....

She looked up at the stallion in the top field, who stood

looking at her. He was immobile, his ears pricked straight up and his eyes fixed on her hands. She really wanted to give him a mint, but she knew that her father would be angry if she caved in and sneaked him one.

She did have some alfalfa pellets in her pocket, so she put down the bucket and walked across the yearling field to the far fence. The stallion grumbled in excitement, his feet dancing at the prospect of a mint.

On her walk over, she had an idea. She would hide a mint in the alfalfa pellets so that if her dad was watching out of the window, she could honestly say that she gave the stallion some pellets.

She fumbled in her pocket, eased out a mint and mixed it in with the pellets. By the time she reached the fence, the stallion was almost beside himself with anticipation. He paced back and forth before diving for her hand, gobbling up all the contents at once.

When the mint hit his taste buds he dissolved into a frenzy of pleasure. He held his head high and curled back his top lip exposing his teeth. A loud sucking noise emitted from his nostrils as he sniffed in the delicate aroma of mint. This display was kept for two major things in life: mares and mints.

Agnes tried hard to get him to stop his exhibition of ecstasy, knowing that if her father saw it, he would know that she had just given the stallion a mint. She turned and looked at the house. She could not see if her father was on his usual staring patrol, so she prayed to God to keep her father away from the window.

On returning to the house, there was no screaming demand for her to go to his office, so she concluded that she had missed the fires of hell, at least for today anyway. As she opened the door, she was greeted by a frenzy of squawking, screeching, whistling and shouting.

"Hello everybody!" Agnes called to the voices.

The voices became louder and more excited. She opened the living room door and smiled at the four parrots jumping up and down on their perches, waiting to be let out. She went from one to the other, opening their doors for the day and gathering up their feed dishes.

They all climbed onto their own little castle turrets and surveyed the universe before them. One at a time, she filled their fruit and veggie dish, poured out fresh seeds and nuts before handing each one a slab of tofu.

Soon the room was quiet again, filled only with the sound of munching and the occasional, "Kiss!" as one of the parrots found a favorite berry or leaf.

The short-lived silence was broken when the kettle whistle started to sound. Agnes had put on the kettle and slipped into the hall to change her forever sodden wet socks. "Kettle, Mother! Kettle, Mother!"

The parrot chorus informed Agnes that the kettle was indeed boiling and that before she made her own tea, she had to make a round of green tea with a tiny drip of honey for all the birds—the morning kettle treat.

Agnes had just settled down to drinking her tea among the parrots, while convincing the cat that suicide was not better than living in a house full of very large inedible birds, when the phone rang. It rang twice, which meant that her father was not at his desk and was probably out. He never let the phone ring, ever. Agnes picked up the phone and listened intently to what was said to her by the voice on the other end. All the parrots fell silent and listened too.

"Sure, I'm sure he won't mind. Yes, bring him around, I'm sure we can help."

She put the phone down and hoped that her father would not hit the roof. Another animal was in need of help and shelter. Since her mother died, Agnes had thrown herself into the farm, raising the horses with her father. She had also begun, not intentionally, to take in injured animals.

The old gypsy man who lived on the edge of the property had taught her the use of herbs and had helped her with the growing collection of misfits and wounded creatures. In return, she cooked and washed for him. Her father was not happy with the arrangement, but Titus, the gypsy, had a way with horses that Agnes's father had never seen the like of elsewhere. He had an eye for good breeding and the business had really taken off since Titus had joined them.

The locals knew to bring strays and injured wild creatures to the Beck Horse Farm: Agnes would always take them in. At only sixteen, she had acquired quite a reputation locally, thanks to Titus and his tall tales over a pint of Guinness.

Agnes went to the house door and banged on the old bell that hung by the coalbunker. That would tell Titus that another injured soul was on its way in. She cleared the kitchen table and scrubbed the surface before putting a clean cloth down.

All the birds began to squawk as a car pulled up. Agnes opened the door before the people could knock. A young girl and her mother stood on the doorstep. The girl had a bundle cradled in her arms that seemed too still and too quiet to be good news.

Titus appeared at the door seconds later and together they all stood around the kitchen table as the young girl unraveled the bundle. There before them lay a raven with most of its top beak ripped off. The bird lay shocked and panting. One eye was half closed and its head twitched uncontrollably. Agnes thanked the people for bringing him here as she herded them to the door.

The parrots sat in total silence, feeling the suffering of the bird that lay on the table. They all sat, deep in their own private memories, remembering the day that they too had come in one by one, as abandoned pets in pain and shock. They too had lain on that table and felt the nimble fingers and minds working to ease their suffering.

Titus looked at the bird from every angle and then scratched his head. The bird was dying. He had to know if the bird wanted to live or be let loose to die. He closed his eyes and saw himself standing beside the bird. The bird, in vision, looked up at him. His eyes pleaded for help. He wanted to fly, to steal, to chase.

That was enough for Titus. He opened his eyes and pulled his bag of tricks towards him. Agnes held the bird gently while Titus clipped off the remains of the beak that was hanging on by a thread. Blood tricked out of the wound. Titus reached for his bag and pulled out silver nitrate sticks that he had stolen from the local vet's office while visiting a long time ago. He knew they would come in handy one day. The stick was dabbed over the wound and the bleeding stopped.

Then he had to address the twitching and the closed eye. Titus guessed it was skull damage. He told Agnes that he was going to have to work in vision, in spirit. Surface healing was not going to be enough to help this bird. Agnes knew what this meant. Immediately she turned off the phones and pulled two chairs up. She would guard against interruptions and Titus would work in vision to put the bird back together again using the deepest healing method that he knew.

Breathing deeply, Titus lit a candle, sat by the bird on the table and closed his eyes. He imagined a flame burning brightly within him and Titus watched as that flame grew bigger and bigger. The flame joined with the candle flame until a wall of fire burned before him. Looking through the fire, he saw faces.

He walked to the fire, joining with the flames as they cleansed and purified him. His intention was to find the Convocation: a gathering of all priests, priestesses and seers. Someone within that gathering would be able to help him. He had done this vision only once before and Titus hoped that he could remember what to do.

He passed through the fire and found himself in a large hall that seemed to stretch beyond the horizon. It was filled to the brim with people and beings of all shapes and sizes who processed around the central flame. Titus stepped out of that flame and found himself in the Convocation. He walked around the central flame that stretched to the ceiling, joining in the eternal vigil kept around the flame of Divinity.

As he walked with the priests and priestesses, Titus noticed that each of the four directions had a beautiful ornate doorway guarded by winged creatures. The guardians watched him watching them as he processed. He was tempted to step out of the procession and look closer at the gates, but he knew that if he delayed, the raven would die. His curiosity would wait for another day. Titus held to the thought of the Raven with the terrible injuries. He could almost hear the raven's thoughts as the bird cried out through all the worlds for help.

It took a few moments for Titus to realize that someone was walking alongside him. The person at his side walked with exactly the same step that he did. Titus stopped and the person stopped. He turned to look and found himself gazing into the eyes of a beautiful priestess.

The priestess was half bird, half human. Her face was that of a young woman, yet instead of hair, her head was crowned with a plumage of brilliant green and golden feathers. Her ample body, part feathers of wild iridescent blues and part dark golden skin, captured Titus's heart. Her wings, tipped with yellows and reds, tucked neatly at her side, and between her low-slung breasts was a tattoo of an X. She held out strong muscular arms to Titus and gripped him hard by the shoulders.

The priestess looked deeply into Titus's eyes and saw the raven. She nodded her head in understanding and motioned that she would help him. Still holding Titus in her grasp, she marched him towards the flame, pushing him through the fire and back into the farmhouse kitchen. Agnes was sitting quietly with her eyes shut. The parrots perched immobile as they watched the priestess walk through the flame. None of them made a sound.

The priestess circled the raven, who tried to reach his head up to see her. The woman motioned for Titus to place his hands on the bird's skull. In vision, Titus placed his hands carefully on the raven's head. The priestess speared into Titus's brain that he must physically touch the bird. Carefully, he placed his physical hands on the bird's head.

The woman's hands rested gently on Titus's shoulder as she guided his brain with her thoughts. Titus felt the raven's skull through his fingertips. The sense of touch was extraordinary as he slowly became aware of a section of the skull that was in the wrong place. It had been pulled forward and was causing a terrible build-up of pressure in the raven's body. Titus began to feel the build-up and his lungs started to struggle.

Very carefully, using the tip of his finger, Titus moved the plate of the skull back to where it belonged. It was hardly even a movement, more of a thought, but the motion was very clear and distinct under his finger. The raven responded immediately by opening the previously closed eye.

The priestess motioned to Titus, showing him that the inner beak was still present but had no outer beak to express itself with. Titus instantly got the message. He imagined a pair of clippers in his hand. Carefully, he removed the inner beak as he had removed the outer beak. The raven shook his head and stretched his neck out as though loosened from a burden.

Next came the deeper work on the brain. The raven's beak had been full of nerve endings and now they were left torn and unfinished. Slowly, as though weaving a web, Titus and the priestess cautiously knotted the nerve endings that had been exposed at the site of the torn beak.

His fingers worked quickly as he followed the nerve lines back up into the bird's brain. With almost an inner sense of touch, Titus searched for torn nerves. When he found them, he reconnected them by using 'inner tools' of the same kind he would have used to restore an electrical wiring system.

Some of the nerves had to be reconnected to a central point in the brain. The injury had unseated many connections and Titus worked furiously to reconnect nerve junctions before they died off. After what seemed an age, the last connection was in place and the central nervous system was restored.

Titus sat back in vision and looked the bird over for any more damage. The bird looked dusty and dirty. Titus tried to look closer, to understand what he was seeing. The priestess moved around to one side of Titus and held her finger out as though she was showing Titus something. He did not understand. She ran her finger across the back of the raven and then held the finger up to Titus. The finger was black with dust. Titus looked blankly at the priestess.

The priestess delved into Titus's memory and found an image that would help. He remembered a time from his early twenties when he was a heavy drinker. He saw how he had become ill and weak from not caring for himself. At that time, he had often seemed dirty when he had looked at himself in the mirror. No matter how hard he had washed, he had always looked grimy. Eventually, his grandmother had told him that he needed what she called a special wash–an inner washing as well as an outer washing.

Titus finally got the message. Out came the inner water spray and cloth. Section by section, Titus washed the bird down, brushing off old feathers and what looked like tiny mites. When he was sure that the bird was clean with no mites, worms or other parasites hidden among the feathers, Titus ran his hand over the back of the bird. He allowed some of his own strength and light to wash over the bird. Not too much, which would potentially kill the bird with the rush of power, but just a little bit, enough to fight through this trauma.

The priestess took her arms from Titus and told him to heal the bird with the dust of the herbs. Titus was confused. He had no clue what the woman was talking about. The priestess became frustrated. She showed him his bag of tinctures and pills and then smacked him around the head. He got the message. Homeopathic remedies: the dust of herbs...of course. Each homeopathic remedy was a massive dilution of a substance so that all that remained of the original ingredient was the equivalent of a fragment, like dust.

The priestess bowed to Titus, who went down on his knee, old-fashioned style, and kissed her hand. It always worked for the ladies, he thought. Gratitude for the help and learning poured out of him as she stepped back onto the flame, her wings held out as the flames licked around her.

Titus opened his eyes and looked at the bird that lay on the table. Both of the raven's eyes were open normally but Titus knew that he would still have to treat the bird homeopathically.

He nudged Agnes, who seemed to have fallen asleep, and told her to get paper, pen, infrared lights and prepare the only spare cage left. While she scurried around with Titus's list, he opened his remedy bag and searched the right substance with his fingertip.

Although he was only tracing through the names of the remedies, something else was happening. The sensitivity that his fingers had acquired while working with the bird priestess had stayed with him. As his fingers ran across the little bottles, his mind was saying, no, not that one, no, not that one. Ah yes, that one.

He looked down at the bottle that had agreed with his finger. Calendula 1m. He took out the bottle and tipped out a small tablet. Crushing it between two spoons, he reduced the tablet to powder before tipping it into the raven's mouth. His fingers returned to the bag and began another journey over the remedies. Titus closed his eyes and allowed his sense of touch to find the follow-up remedies that would be needed over the next few days. One by one, he took out bottles without looking at them.

He lined up the bottles first, then he looked to see what it was that he had picked. Hypericum, Silicea, Symphytum, Sulphur. His eyebrows rose when he read the names: all ones that he would have chosen consciously to aid in the rehabilitation of the raven over the next ten days. He smiled at his newly found skill and quietly thanked the bird priestess once more for the wonderful gift.

Agnes panted as she returned with bags of bedding, lights and paper. The pen was gripped firmly in her teeth. Quickly, she set up the only remaining spare cage, which was thankfully large and able to accommodate the raven comfortably. The infrared lights were rigged up to shine heat into the cage and bedding was spread along the floor. Titus gently picked up the raven, who by now was breathing normally and had both eyes wide open. He sat calmly in Titus's hands and visibly relaxed once the red heat was on him as he rested in his cage. The bird looked at Titus and Titus looked back at him.

In his mind, Titus tried to show the bird that although he would never be able to return to the wild, he would not have a life of cages either. He would have the sky, the trees and grass once again, with Agnes to prepare food for him and protect him.

The raven showed Titus an image that would haunt him for the rest of his life. Through his mind, the raven showed himself guarding the land. At first, Titus could not see what there was to guard. So the raven looked deeper into the earth and showed Titus what he was truly guarding.

Deep within the earth was a gigantic man in a timeless profound sleep. His hair grew into the rock, his nails grew into the earth and his beard was home to many small creatures and insects.

This sleeper dreamed the world, holding all the birds and animals in life as he slept. And the raven's task was to guard and protect the sleeper from being awakened.

The raven looked sorrowfully at Titus as he showed his human helper that he could no longer protect the sleeper without a beak. Titus, in his imagination, asked the raven if he could make a noise. He showed the bird a vision of himself shouting. The raven, after a short breath of confusion, got the idea. He could not attack with his beak, but he could sound the alarm for all the other ravens.

With that, the raven made a terrible shrieking and cawing noise that caused Agnes to place her hands over her ears. Titus grinned as all the parrots, who up to now had been wonderfully quiet, joined in the screeching with their own noisy opera.

It seemed that the farm had acquired a new alarm system.

ABOUT THIS BOOK

In this collection of nine magical tales, British teacher and priestess Josephine Dunne follows in the noble tradition of Dion Fortune in communicating esoteric wisdom through stories. While these lively tales are entertaining in and of themselves, they also convey a deeper perspective to those willing to look.

Josephine's stories touch on a broad range of themes, from faeries to exorcism to the healing of animals. Her spiritual insight and deep knowledge of human nature runs throughout.

These tales educate the imagination, and offer much guidance for those pursuing a path of magical initiation.

ABOUT THE AUTHOR

Josephine McCarthy is an Irish foreign born national who grew up in northern Britain. She is a respected magical adept and author of numerous books on magic including classics such *The Exorcists Handbook, The Magical Knowledge Trilogy,* and *The Book of Gates: A Magical Translation.* She is the designer and author of the Quareia Magicians Deck, and designer, artist and author of the Mystagogus Divination Deck and book. She is also the sole author and school director of the Quareia Magical training course.